THE
POLYMATH

A Screenplay
By

MOURAD MOURAD

EARTH Pictures

Photos Credits
EARTH Pictures

British Library Cataloguing-in-Publication Data
A catalogue record for this book is available from the British
Library and the Lebanese National Library

Designed and printed by EARTH Pictures

Published by
EARTH Pictures Ltd
Registered in England and Wales
Registration Number: 08581401

The Polymath
A Screenplay

Mourad Mourad

was born in 1978 and raised in Ras Nhach, Batroun
(Lebanon). British – Lebanese Author, Philosopher,
Journalist and Climate Activist who is well travelled
around the world.

He is the Author of *Mesopotamia 681*,
Our Path To Eternity, Death at Dawn and *On The
Cross*.

THE POLYMATH

Caption

In the 12th century AD, Muslim civilization had reached its peak. In Andalusia, a diverse society thrived, one that welcomed the light of justice, knowledge, philosophy and science. But this paradise did not last long before Muslims fell dramatically into the trap of organized religion.

The rest of Europe was living some of its darkest days. Called into battle by the pope, Christian crusaders pillaged the holy land, provoking Muslim extremism. Each side claimed to act in the name of God, as if the creator was ever the exclusive property of one of those religions.

One man favored philosophy over organized religion. He introduced the world to a new way of knowing God.

Ext. Atlantic coast - Day

Andalusia. Southwestern Spain. Averroes, (60s), stands on a rocky outcrop, looking out at the sea as gulls gather around him. We see him from behind, his white hair and white linen robes dance in the gentle breeze. The black rocks are stark against the blue sky and green Atlantic.

Superimpose: Andalusia - 1184 ad

closeup - bread in his hand.

Averroes

wars, wars, wars. When will the greed of human beings end? Is it for the sake of God? For the sake of humanity? No. For the sake of the rulers' egos. Yes, that's what it's about. By invasions and bloodshed, they write their names in history. Our caliph forgot that God said "Do not transgress. God does not like transgressors. "

As we pull back from Averroes, he throws pieces of bread to the gulls. We leave the man and sweep through the dry Andalusian countryside, arriving finally at Santarem, in Portugal.

Ext. Santarem battlefield - Day

Caption: Santarem, Portugal.

The Almohad army lays siege to the hilltop fortress of Santarem, built on a bend in the Tagus River. Soldiers of king Alfonso I (75) defend their city from the high walls, but struggle under the heavy arrows and weaponry of the attackers.

The Almohad caliph Abu Yaqub Yusuf (49) and his son Abu Yusuf Yaqub (mid-20s) stand in front of their tent watching the battle.

Abu Yusuf

their resistance is getting weaker.

Abu Yaqub

Santarem will soon fall. We've easily gained the upper hand.

Abu Yaqub looks up the hill, where Almohad soldiers have succeeded in setting up armored protective huts and are preparing ladders in order to climb the castle walls. Near the gates of the city, a group of soldiers prepares a battering ram. Other soldiers surround the tent, waiting patiently for orders. Abu Yaqub carefully considers the idle soldiers.

Abu Yaqub

We don't need our entire army to invade the city. Take half of our men and attack Lisbon.

Abu Yusuf

Yes Mulana/our leader.

Int. Santarem castle keep - Day

Alfonso I of Portugal looks out the window of a watchtower inside of the castle keep in the city of Santarem. He observes the Almohad army surrounding the castle, moving war machines into place. His own soldiers, protected by the city walls, shoot arrows from time to time, but they have the fear of defeat in their eyes. Below, in the city square, townspeople are gathered, silently awaiting their fate. In spite of this, Alfonso has a confident look on his face, for he is also watching half of the Almohad army as they move off in the direction of Lisbon.

An old priest (80s), frail and scared, approaches Alfonso I from behind.

Priest

The people are afraid the city could fall tomorrow, my lord.

Alfonso

We only need to hold our ground until help arrives.

Priest

Help?

Alfonso

I sent a messenger to my son-in-law Ferdinand II of Leon. I hope that they arrive at the right moment... And half of the Caliph's army has just left for some reason.

Alfonso shouts encouragement to his men.

Night falls as the Almohad army continues their siege.

Ext. Santarem city gates – Day

The following morning the city gates fell. The Almohad army fights at the gates of the city and chaos reigns. Portuguese soldiers fight fiercely, but they are quickly losing ground.

Int. Castle keep - Day

Alfonso, standing high in the castle keep, looks out at the horizon and smiles.

Ext. Santarem city gates - Day

The Caliph Abu Yaqub, astride his horse, shouts commands to his men, fighting their way to the gates.

Suddenly the army of Ferdinand II appears behind the Almohad army.

Ferdinand II of Leon points his sword commanding his army to ride at maximum speed into the heart of the Almohad army. They clash fiercely, slaying the Almohad soldiers by the dozen.

The caliph Abu Yaqub spins his horse, turning in confusion. He shouts at his men to keep attacking but he himself is already defeated in his disbelief. An archer on the city wall raises his crossbow and shoots the caliph in the neck. He falls from his horse instantaneously.

Inter title: "Actor's name" in

The Polymath

Ext. Forest - Day

Eight knights gallop through a forest in northern Italy. They are knights of templar, and their armor bears the Maltese cross. Among them is Robert (30s) of St. Albans, an English templar, bearded. His face has been hardened by battle, and yet clear eyes of an educated and compassionate man.

Ext. Medieval city of Verona - Day

Title: Verona: papal residence

Six of the templar knights ride through the city and arrive at the gates of the papal residence. They enter. We see the symbol of the papacy.

Ext. Rocky coast - Night

Robert and another knight arrive riding one horse at a rocky coast in the north of France. A rough wooden boat awaits them in a cave. They board their horse and push out into the calm sea. Night turns to day, and the sun shines as they arrive on the English shore.

Int. Beaumont palace tower - Day

Ronald, adviser to the king of England watches over the misty moors from a window as Robert and the other knight ride towards the palace. He turns to leave for the throne room.

Int. Beaumont palace throne room - Day

The throne room of King Henry II (51) is dark and rough, hewn wooden beams hold up the floors and heavy tapestries hang, barely keeping out the cold.

Ronald enters.

Ronald

Your grace, Robert of St. Albans has just returned from Jerusalem.

King Henry II stands.

Henry II

Bring him in.

Guards move aside, and the two knights templar enter. Robert is carrying an ancient white book. He kneels to one knee before the king, offering it to him.

Henry II

welcome back my most valuable eyes. Tell me of Jerusalem and the search in Solomon's temple. It seems you have brought something with you.

(To the guards) leave us alone and shut the door.

The guards and the adviser leave.

Robert

Your grace, I did my best to bring you something of value. Our small band of templars found a chest, destroyed but carefully hidden. In it there were two books, one black and one white. The black book was still in good condition. But as you can see (opening the white book) only a few pages at the end of this one are still legible.

Henry takes the book and examines it.

Henry II

I suppose the black book was taken to the pope (Robert nods). Did you manage to look at it?

Robert

It's written in Syriac, but we were fortunate to have among us a templar who speaks the language. The title of the book is: Power and wealth.

Henry II

(holding up the white book) And what is the title of this one?

Robert

God only knows. Among us we spoke Syriac, Hebrew, Latin and Arabic, but it's written in a language no one recognized. Since it was in such a bad condition the others were not interested. But look at this.

He shows the king a faint drawing near the end of the book of a hexagon surrounded by six planet-like spheres. Henry nods with interest.

Henry II

We will see what the scholars of England can make of it. Tell me what is happening in Jerusalem?

Robert

We are destroying human civilization by waging such a war. The franks are barbaric. Before the pope declared this war, Muslims, Christians and Jews of the holy land were living in peace among each other.

Henry II

You know very well that I do not believe in these crusades. But we must send some troops, so everything is not left in the hands of other kingdoms.

Robert

I hope you are not sending me back there.

Henry II

No, not at this moment. I have something different for you. I have received word that Alfonso of Portugal defeated the Almohad army at Santarem. He was saved at the last moment by Ferdinand of Spain. The caliph Abu Yaqub was killed in the battle. His army retreated to Seville.

Robert listens intently.

Henry II

The Spanish and the Portuguese kings will certainly get the blessing of the pope in such a victory against the Muslims. You know that I am trying to minimize influence of the pope here in England, but such victories will awaken the zealots in our lands. I'm concerned that the death of the caliph could weaken Muslim influence in Andalusia.

Robert

But your daughter is married to the king of Castile.

Henry II

When I accepted the marriage of Eleanor to the Castilian king, I expected to influence his loyalties. But the power of the pope continues to grow on the Iberian Peninsula, and my daughter has alienated me.

Robert

It will be disastrous if the church gains further influence in Spain. How do you think we should face that?

Henry II

I would like you to go to Andalusia. Go and see. Find out how they are dealing with the defeat. Who is the new caliph? How are the people living? What is the atmosphere?

Robert

I will gladly go as long as it's not an order to fight on behalf of the pope and his church.

Henry pats Robert firmly on the shoulder as they laugh.

Ext. La Giralda square - Day - Continuous

Abu Yusuf Yaqub, son of the slain caliph, rides his horse solemnly towards into the city square, at the head of the defeated Almohad army. Soldiers carry on their shoulders a white structure of billowing white cloth. Inside is the body of the caliph, wrapped in a shroud.

They arrive to the city square in central Seville in front of la Giralda mosque. Crowds of people gathered. Some search frantically for their husbands and sons, returning from war. Others surround the soldiers who protect the body of the caliph, crying and mourning their leader. The caravan moves solemnly through the crowd.

A man in an intricate black dress embroidered with gold emerges from the crowd. It is Averroes, dignified, blue eyes gazing compassionately, white hair falling soft around his face. Soldiers step aside upon seeing him and let him approach. Abu Yussuf dismounts and as the two men embrace, tears form in their eyes.

Abu Yusuf

My father the caliph is gone.

Averroes

Be strong now. We mourn him as much as you. We have lost a great leader.

Abu Yusuf

Why would God allow for such humiliation? We pray for him, why has he abandoned us in battle?

Averroes

God does everything for a reason. I warned your father against this attack, but he, may his soul rest in peace, did not take my advice. Now the land needs a new leader. Show the people that you are the man they need.

Abu Yusuf

I will avenge my father's death.

Averroes

Calm now... It is not the right moment to think of vengeance. Let us now think of the funeral.

Abu Yusuf takes Averroes by the hand, holding the reigns in the other. They continue towards the palace.

Abu Yusuf

I will not bury him here. He always wished to be buried in Tinmel in Marrakesh

Averroes

That is no problem. We must hold the coronation ceremony and then tomorrow you can bring him there.

Abu Yusuf climbs on his horse, he leaves the square, and his soldiers follow.

Averroes steps up onto the ledge of a fountain in the middle of the square and waves a signal to his student Yazeed (20s) who turns it off. The water quiets, and so does the crowd, turning towards Averroes to hear him speak.

Averroes

We are all saddened by the tragic loss of our caliph, Mulana Abu Yaqub. But life must go on. The elders of Andalusia will crown the new caliph this evening. Come pray with us at dawn to say farewell to our beloved leader. May God bless you, and may his peace and mercy be on you.

Int. Caliphs palace throne room - Night

The coronation of the new caliph, Abu Yusuf Yaqub (henceforth referred to as the caliph.)

Senior community figures, scholars, army chiefs, ladies of the court, religious leaders and judges gather in the palace hall, a luxurious and light-filled room of white arabesque arches and fine silks.

Averroes

The community elite of Andalusia are proud to proclaim you Mulana Abu Yusuf Yaqub, new caliph of the Almohad kingdom.

The crowd applauds. Abu Yusuf sits on the throne and Averroes crowns him with the caliph's turban, which has a large diamond on top.

Ext. La Giralda square - Dawn

The body of the caliph is on display in the square in front of la Giralda mosque. Averroes leads the prayer dressed in white with a light blue cloak. We notice for the first time the diversity of the citizens of Seville. Muslims, Christians, and Jews are differentiated by the clothes they wear. They are ethnically diverse as well, a cosmopolitan mix of scholars, merchants, and families having relocated to Seville from all over the caliphate.

Averroes

"O god, forgive our living and our dead, those who are present among us and those who are absent, our young and our old, our males and our females. O god, if our dead man was a doer of good then increase his good deeds, and if he was a wrongdoer, then overlook his bad deeds. O god, forgive him and have mercy on him, keep him safe and sound and forgive him, honor his rest and ease his entrance; wash him with water and snow and hail, and cleanse him of sin as a white garment is cleansed of dirt. O god, give him a home better than his home and a family better than his family. O god, admit him to paradise and protect him from the torment of the grave and the torment of hellfire; make his grave spacious and fill it with light.

" Then praise the almighty. God is the greatest. God is the greatest. God is the greatest".

(turning head to right) Peace be upon you. (to left) Peace be upon you.

The sun shines clearly in the sky, erasing the darkness of the night.

Ext. Caliphs palace gates - Day

Abu Yusuf, his family and his entourage are gathered for departure for Marrakesh. The new caliph turns to Averroes.

Caliph

I leave Andalusia in your hands wise man, until I return from Marrakesh. Commander Abu Yahya takes care of the defense of the northern borders.

Averroes touches the hair of Al-Nasir (9), the son of the caliph, who in turn embraces the wise man.

Averroes

Do not worry. I will manage the kingdom until you return. May God protect you. Have a safe trip.

The caravan, including the body of the caliph, leaves the city, headed by a small army.

Ext. Robert's cottage - Day

Robert of St. Albans takes leave outside the medieval cottage of his family. It is small and comfortable, a stone house with a thatched roof and pigs and chickens running around the fenced courtyard. Tears flood down his sister Camilla's (16) face.

Robert

Do not cry. I promise to return in just a few months. I'm not going far this time. (turning to his uncle) you take care of her well, uncle. Since the death of our mother, she has no one.

Aunt

Do not worry about your sister. Camilla is a brilliant girl, and we will ensure she continues her education.

Robert embraces each member of his family, mounts his horse and leaves.

Int. Caliphs palace lecture hall - Night

A grand lecture hall in the palace, white walls and arabesque arches intricately carved in with Arabic script. Tiles decorate the walls and floors. Hundreds of metal and glass lamps light the room with a warm orange glow.

Students sit at low, delicate wooden tables, some quietly discussing their academic subject, others reading from texts, still others writing in large parchment volumes.

At the front of the room on a small platform sits Averroes. On his left an ancient volume is propped in an inlaid Rehal, and he writes in a volume which sits on a table to his right. He mumbles to himself softly as he works.

Averroes

I disagree with you completely, my brother, Aristotle. You say, "a friend to all is a friend to none, " and I say I don't believe in this exclusive kind of relationship between human beings.

(looking out at his students they work)

Humanity should live as one family and therefore each one of us must love everybody and be honest and friendly with everyone. Maybe society during your days was different than now, but... Now... Friendship is a chance that wise people should offer to the entire society because such connection can help less fortunate people to be influenced by new types of knowledge and experience. The best way to build human societies is through love, sharing and understanding. This is the right path that makes human civilization flourish...

Ext. Tours forest - Night

Caption: Tours, France

While Andalusia flourishes in the light of intellectual illumination, the rest of Europe is embroiled in pestilence, war, and fanaticism. It is truly the dark ages. France has already come under the yolk of the inquisition, and people live in fear of the tyranny of the church.

In a dark forest near tours, two young peasant women Annabelle and Christine (20s) and a dog make their way cautiously. Only their oil lamp lights the way until they come to a small cottage. They wave goodbye to each other at the front door.

Annabelle

be careful on your return. Thank you for walking me home.

Christine

Don't worry about me. Good night, Annabelle.

The dog barks at some bushes beside the house. The friend calls the dog, and they leave.

Int. Cottage - Night - Continuous

Annabelle, alone in her bedroom, lights a lamp. She slips out of her dress, revealing her beautiful curves in the soft light.

We see all of this through a hole in the wooden shutter: someone is peeping in on her.

Ext. Cottage - Night - Continuous

The voyeur moves towards the front door, only a dark shadow in the night. His middle-aged hand, thin and bony reaches for the door handle.

Int. Cottage - Night - Continuous

Annabelle hears the door opening and reaches for her robe. She knows who it is but cannot believe that he would enter her house like this.

A priest, Father Laurent (50s) appears in the doorway. Annabelle stares at him, eyes wide with fear and anger.

Annabelle

Why are you following me?

The priest takes a step towards her.

Annabelle

Do not touch me. Don't you dare.

The priest advances quickly now, undoing his garment and grabbing at the young woman's robe. She screams and slaps him in the face. He is stunned and grabs her again, but she slips past him and runs out the door. He stands alone in the room, her robe in his hands.

Ext. Tours forest - Night - Continuous

The frightened and naked Annabelle runs through the forest hoping to catch up to her friend still on the road.

Annabelle

Christine! Christine! Help me! Help me!

In the distance Christine calls Annabelle. A light appears through the trees and Annabelle runs towards it.

Int. Tours church - Night - Continuous

The priest enters the nearby church, where his holy brothers are dining together.

Father Laurent

There is a whore walking through the forest naked. I saw her with my own eyes, and I turned away with such shame and came straight to you. We must arrest her.

The men stand, ready to exact justice.

Ext. Tours forest - Night - Continuous

The two young women run through the forest towards Christine's home, their little lamp lighting their way. Annabelles bare feet, ripped up by brambles, slow their progress.

Christine is holding the naked and shivering Annabelle. She has taken off her top and is wrapped around Annabelle's waist.

Soon the priests are upon them, torches in hand. Christines dog barks fiercely as they approach. The girls cower as the men circle them. The dogs barking becomes furious, and Father Laurent begins hitting him with his torch. The others join until the dog is dead.

Father Laurent

The greatest sin! Oh lord Jesus please forgive my eyes for seeing these women together! You whores! You witches!

The priests catch the two girls and are led away. Annabelle spits in the face of Father Laurent.

Int. Tours dungeon - Night - Continuous

The two girls are thrown into a dungeon, filled with the stench and filth of prisoners, and cries of the tortured.

Int. Caliphs palace throne room - Night

Averroes wraps up a meeting with fellow politicians and returns to his chambers.

Int. Caliphs palace Averroes chambers - Night

Averroes enters his chambers, deep within the palace. He feeds his cats. He passes by his daughter Rabab's (25) room. She is reading a book and yawning.

Int. Rababs room - Night

Averroes

(kissing her forehead) You need to get some rest. We have a busy day tomorrow.

Rabab

I'll sleep father. But you need to sleep as well. You are the one who needs rest, being a judge, a teacher, a philosopher, an imam, a physician. Promise me you will go to bed and not stay up to write some mad treatise on how to create harmony between cats and mice.

Averroes

(winking)

I can't promise you anything. Life is too short and there are many things we should do.

A cat jumps onto the bed and they both pet it, then Averroes takes his leave.

Int. Averroes bedroom - Night

He crawls in bed, and he falls asleep while reading.

Ext. Tours city square - Day

The town is gathered to witness yet another "trial" and execution. Two women and one man are tied to a huge wooden column in the middle of a pyre.

Robert, on his way to Seville, rides into town just as the father Laurent is announcing the judgment of the inquisition.

Father Laurent

The church has opened an inquisition into the crimes of three corrupt citizens of our society. Annabelle LeBoeuf and Christine LeGrande, have committed the sin of lesbianism, as witnessed by members of the clergy.

The crowd jeers at the two women, bound and barely clothed. The men in the crowd spit upon them lasciviously, eyes devouring their flesh. The women leer in disgust. A bank of nuns stands stoically observing.

Father Laurent

Monsieur Jerome petit is accused of heresy, guilty of owning a range of Islamic, philosophic and scientific books. He is a threat to our society and a servant of the anti-Christ.

The crowd roars again, some holding up wooden crosses, others turning their eyes towards heaven in supplication.

Father Laurent

the inquisition of the church of tours has found the three accused guilty and punishes them to death by fire. Father Laurent gives a signal, and four executioners step forward with torches to set the fire.

Robert, who has been watching the spectacle, forces his way inside the circle, surprised and angry.

Robert

Stop!

The executioners, the priests and the crowd become silent with surprise.

Father Laurent

Who are you to stop the judgment of the church?

Robert

And who are you to claim to be representatives of the almighty on earth? If Jesus was among you today, would he allow such cruelty?

Father Laurent

(turning to the guards)

Get this heretic out of my sight! Arrest him.

The executioners continue setting their fires. Ten guards step to surround Robert, who draws his sword. Flames begin to devour the bodies of the three accused, who scream in pain. Robert closes his eyes

Mourad Mourad

in rage, and then explodes in anger. His horse rears and Robert turns him to escape the town. He breaks through the barrier of guards and jumps over the priest, who falls to the ground, hitting his head on a rock and dying instantly.

Robert rides at top speed to the edge of town and into the forest.

Int. Caliphs palace lecture hall - Day

Averroes is lecturing philosophy and religion students about al Ghazali's book the incoherence of the philosophers. They sit in rapt attention.

Averroes

(holding up two volumes that he has written)

And here is my response to al Ghazali's "The incoherence of the philosophers". (smiling mischievously) It's called "The incoherence of the incoherence!"

The students laugh and applaud, speaking among themselves. Yazeed, the young protege of Averroes, and one of his brightest students, raises his hand.

Averroes

Yes Yazeed, tell me what you think.

28

Yazeed

First, I like the title. I imagine you are giving thee the punch they deserve.

Averroes is amused and the class laughs.

Yazeed

I would like to know when we can read the book, and when the process of copying it will begin.

Averroes

I am as eager as you, and I am looking forward to hearing how you all receive what I have written. The book is ready from tonight and it is yours.

An Italian student, Alessandro (30) raises his hand.

Alessandro

And is it to be translated into Latin and other languages?

Averroes

of course. These ideas must be allowed to fly to every house on earth. There is no method more effective than translation to destroy the barriers between lands. As a representative of Genoa, it is your duty to share and exchange information with your fellow Latin speakers. (turning to the others) and each of you has the duty to bring this knowledge to your people!

Averroes turns towards a group of young students. He is surprised to notice a new face among them, Ruqaya (20) an African woman wearing a veil. Ruqaya is quiet and unaccustomed to being spoken to by people outside of her family.

Averroes

A new face! It seems we welcome a new student today!

Ruqaya smiles shyly and her eyes flick up to Averroes, but she quickly averts them. Next to her sits another female student Rawya (20), who helps her out.

Rawya

Yes master, this is Ruqaya. She recently arrived with her family from Nubia.

Averroes

welcome Ruqaya. We are honored to have you here with us. No need to be shy. Relax, I would like to hear your voice. Tell me what is your impression after your first lecture?

Ruqaya remains mute. Rawya encourages her to answer. After a long silence she begins in a small voice.

Ruqaya

I am sorry I am so shy. This is the first time I am in a school where men sit next to women. It's the first time I sit in a public place with unveiled ladies. I do believe it's the only place on earth to allow such a thing!

Averroes comes closer to the young woman.

Averroes

And what have you witnessed here? Misconduct between our students? Assaults on the women by the men?

Ruqaya

No...

Averroes

Of course not. Because all of our students are interested only in learning things. Thats why they're here. I thank God, day and night for such enthusiastic scholars. And to be frank (he leans in conspiratorially) I learn from them the same way they learn from me.

Ruqaya whispers something in Rawya's ear.

Rawya

Ruqaya has a question, but she doesn't dare ask.

Averroes laughs out loud.

Averroes

What is it, Ruqaya? Please ask it yourself.

Averroes makes a grand show of checking his clothes.

Averroes

Look, I have no sword, no knife. (putting his hand on her shoulder) You are in a new world. Enjoy the space and freedom! Remove fear and restrictions of the past and look with self-assurance towards the future.

Quiet admiration appears in Ruqaya's eyes and finally she speaks.

Ruqaya

You are the famous savant and philosopher Averroes and I have heard so much about you. But you are also an imam, a Muslim scholar and that means you know very well our laws. So how do you allow women to not wear veils? We learned that the veil is an obligation in our religion, is it not? What about the verse that says "O prophet, tell your wives and your daughters and the women of the believers to bring down over themselves [part] of their outer garments. That is more suitable that they will be not known and not be hurt. "

Averroes

When the prophet died, the religious scholars started to re-interpret messages he received from God. They told us that women should be covered so as not to be desired by men. But that's not it at all! Islam was such a revolutionary idea and at the beginning the community of Muslims had enemies everywhere and so it was better if they were covered so no one would recognize them. It was for their safety, so they could go out in public, because all of the women at the time were covered. They could blend in.

(laughing) even myself, everyone in this town knows me! Sometimes I wear a farmer's cloak so that I can get my shopping done in peace! And why must you cover your hair? It's not an accessory that you buy to look beautiful and attract men. Hair is made by God, it's natural. Please stop thinking about things from such a low point of view.

Ruqaya ponders all he has said and seems satisfied.

Averroes

Your outward appearance never reflects your true belief. Only the heart does. God sees what is in your heart, not your dress. These so-called scholars try their best to make women feel they are weak... Paranoid, as if they were the eternal target for sexual male monsters. Listen to this verse from Surat Aaraf "O children of Adam, we have bestowed upon you clothing to conceal your private parts and as adornment. But the clothing of righteousness - that is best. That is from the signs of God that perhaps they will remember". You see how this verse separates clothing that covers the body and clothes of the soul. Both are something you can choose to wear, but God only sees what's in your soul.

Ruqaya smiles and leans against Rawya.

Ruqaya

How lucky you are to have the great Averroes in your lives!

Averroes

Now you are here with us. Enjoy your time and fill it with useful deeds like aiding the helpless, learning new skills, reading, writing, praying... Use your imagination, set your soul free from restrictions. Have no fear as long as you trust in God, because his love has no limits.

Averroes puts his hand on Rawya's shoulder.

Averroes

Rawya is one of my brightest students. I'm sure she will help you adapt to this new environment.

Ext. Seville streets - Day

the narrow streets of Seville, empty in the midday sun. A figure wearing a burqa, a head-to-toe covering for women, quietly hurries down the street. The figure comes to a door. A knock on the door and a beautiful woman, Amira

(38) opens to warmly greet the visitor. The figure enters and they shut the door behind them. Two small toddlers play on the floor. He throws off the burqa, revealing that it is in fact a man, Ahmad (40s). The two embrace passionately.

Int. Abu Omar's house - Day

Inside their cool living room, Abu Omar (60s) sits on a sofa gently massaging the body of his disabled wife Um Omar (60s). They are listening to their son Omar (28) play his rebab. Their daughter, Rawya is studying. Omar finishes his piece, and the small family applauds.

Abu Omar

Great, my son. When do you play at the palace then?

Omar

Next Saturday after the evening prayer.

Um Omar

I wish I could attend but you know my situation.

Abu Omar

You will attend. I will rent a wagon and take you there. Rawya can arrange a sofa for you at the palace, (turning to his daughter) can't you?

Rawya

I will try. I am sure Averroes won't mind.

Abu Omar tenderly picks up his wife and carries her into the bedroom, where he lays her in the prepared bed. He sits on the edge and gives her some liquid medication. She touches his face filled with respect and gratitude. He smiles lovingly at her.

Um Omar

I am sorry that I am no longer able to fulfill your body's needs. It's now been five years since the beginning of my illness.

Abu Omar

Never mind that. I'm an old man, my desire is not as it used to be.

Um Omar

I want you to be happy. I really do.

Abu Omar

I am happy. (kisses her.)

Um Omar

My love. If you want to marry a second wife, I will understand.

Abu Omar

I love only one woman, and that's you. Marrying a second wife would satisfy my sexual desires... But it would be wrong because I would not love her, and every human being has the right to be loved.

He hugs her and tears appear in both their eyes.

Ext. Bordeaux city center - Night

Robert rides into the city center in Bordeaux. The streets are lively with people and lit with torches. He slows in front of the cathedral and looks around until he spots a small cottage. He dismounts and knocks on the door, but there is no answer. A woman (50s) sits weaving a basket, bathed in light from a torch hanging from the cathedral.

Woman

Yes, my son? Can I help you?

Robert

I'm looking for Sister Magdalene.

Woman

She is not home now. Wait for her a while. She will be leaving the cathedral shortly.

Robert sits on a stone near the door of the cottage. He waits long enough for the woman to finish two baskets. A group of nuns leaves the cathedral, among them the one called Magdalene. She says farewell to the other nuns and approaches the cottage. Robert says in a quiet voice:

Robert

Shalom Sarah.

Startled, the woman stops.

Sarah

Who are you? What do you want? Please, keep your voice down.

Robert pulls a small box from his pocket.

Robert

A small gift from King Henry the II.

Sarah takes the box, and opens it and peers inside. Upon seeing its contents, she looks up to Robert with new trust, having understood that he is a friend.

Sarah

You cannot come in now. People will gossip. Come back at midnight. Make sure no one sees you.

Int. Ahmad's house - Night

Ahmad, the man who wore the burqa, sits at the dinner table with his wife, Farida (40s) and their daughter (19) and three sons (15,) (14) and (12). Farida serves each of her family members. She looks with suspicion at her husband, who eats quickly, as if he had not eaten for ages. She shakes her head and slowly begins chewing her food. She moves her foot towards Ahmad's under the table and gently caresses his leg. Ahmad continues eating, not looking up from his plate.

Ahmad

I am very tired; I had a tough day in the market. I think I'll go to bed just after dinner.

Farida looks at him with anger and disappointment, but he continues eating.

Int. Sarah's house - Night

Sarah and Robert sit inside of her house in the quiet night, the windows closed to prying eyes.

Robert

You are very brave to risk your life as a spy in the church. The king told me you are a wealthy woman. If you do not do this for money, then why?

Sarah

Money means nothing when the cause you are fighting for is noble. My goal is to fulfill my covenant with God and protect human lives, everything else is minuscule. As a Jew, it is my duty to protect my people from the church's persecution, and to know the future plans of the pope, there is nothing better than working in one of the most important cathedrals in France.

She looks down into the box that Robert gave her when they met outside. It contains an inverted cross, a jeweled star of David and a crescent.

Sarah

I understand the king's message, but I have no time to go the Andalusia now, not before the end of the month.

Robert

King Henry told me you could help me get into the city.

Sarah

(carefully considering) Well, I have always trusted king's intentions in the region. When I came here to Bordeaux it was at the forefront of the inquisition. But I understand that now the center has changed. It's true that here, perhaps it is too late. But if we can be of help in Andalusia... We must go there. I must find an excuse to give to the clergy and find others to fulfill my duties. I don't want to burn my bridges here; my connections might prove to be useful in the future.

Her demeanor has changed, from one of welcome to one of weariness.

Robert

How is the situation here? There is worry in your eyes.

Sarah

Terror would be the word. The pope is planning on expanding his inquisition outside the borders of France. All other Christian kingdoms and states will soon be under the savage judgment of the clergy. Torturing innocents will be the norm. They will control the land from sea to sea. I see darkness in the future.

Robert

I too have witnessed their savagery.

Sarah

Perhaps our hope lies with England. As an island, it can distance herself from the church.

Robert

I believe that the Muslims are our hope in defeating the church. You the Jews are educated but your population is small. You have money but no military power.

Sarah

The only safe place for free people is Andalusia. As for the rest of the Islamic kingdoms, we are receiving disturbing news. Extremist groups have taken the upper hand, and their popularity is growing every day. Unfortunately, I believe it's a natural reaction to the attacks of the crusaders. Extremism on one side gives birth to extremism on the other.

Robert

So, do you have permission to enter Seville?

Sarah

Yes. I have the codes given only to friends of the Almohad. Don't worry, you will be there as my guest. You will stay at my house and eat my food. Tomorrow, we travel. I will go by wagon, and you must ride at a distance from me so as not to arouse suspicion. Once we reach Barchanona we will be able to continue together. There Magdalene disappears, and I become once again Sarah. And you become my driver.

Sarah rises and goes to a cupboard, pulling out two goblets and wine. She pours some for each of them and they toast.

Ext. Caliphs palace garden - Day

Morning in the palace gardens, a veritable paradise. Palm trees and jasmine, figs and pomegranates, tile-covered fountains, reflecting pools, shade dapples the warm hazy light.

Averroes paces seven students: Alessandro, David, Philippe, Dalia, Jose, Rabab and Yazeed, who sit in the shade on stones, treating books and scrolls. A small silver tray full of delicate cookies and tea sits, untouched near the young scholars.

Abu Yahya (50s), chief of the Almohad Andalusian army interrupts the scene. He is a sturdy man who has seen many battles. He grabs a hand full of cookies and shoves one into his mouth.

Abu Yahya

Good morning, wise man.

Though annoyed at being disturbed, Averroes forces a bright smile.

Averroes

(with mock enthusiasm) Good morning, strong man.

Averroes makes an exaggerated eating motion to a servant, who runs off to bring breakfast. The two men walk through the garden as servants bring out blankets and pillows, and then trays of tea and sweets.

Averroes

How's the situation at the borders?

Abu Yahya

All is calm. And how are things with your classes?

Averroes

I am blessed to have such brilliant students coming from so many places. Yazeed and my daughter are the only locals.

Abu Yahya

I should like to meet such savants.

Averroes

(pedantically pointing) That is Alessandro from Genoa. He translates my work into Latin. And there is Philip of Toulouse, into Frankish. Jose into Castilian. David of the English isles translates into English. And Dalia from Marrakesh into Hebrew.

Abu Yahya

(Munching on another cookie.)

That's amazing.

Averroes

This is my vision of the future of mankind; people from all backgrounds working as one. No more of your wars and divisions. I hope you're looking forward to your retirement!

Averroes and Abu Yahya join the students and three servants arrive with a lavish feast.

Averroes

It's time for a break. When the stomach is hungry the mind gets lost.

The students put aside their books and tuck into the feast. They pour tea and talk, laughing in the shade of the trees. A musician plays music in the distance, adding luxury to the morning.

As they finish their break, a messenger arrives. He has the dirt of the road in his clothes. Abu Yahya rises to meet him; Averroes grabs some tea to offer. The three men leave the group of students.

Averroes

Tell us. You have a sense of urgency.

Messenger

The Almoravids are attacking Marrakesh from the south and east. I've been sent to tell you we need more troops in Africa as soon as possible.

Abu Yahya

We cannot leave the north without protection. We just lost the war in Portugal so the morale of the Christian kingdoms is high, and they may attack at any moment.

Averroes

We have to keep a strong defensive line at the northern borders, so you'd better send the local officers to Marrakesh.

Abu Yahya

(sarcastic)

Oh, I see you are a war expert, too ... Yes, I was thinking the same. We will send a large faction from Cordoba, and half of the officers from each surrounding city. Let us hope that news from Morocco does not reach our northern enemies.

Ext. Ahmad's house - Day

Ahmad leaves his house with a large bag. His wife follows him from a distance. He disappears behind a boulder and a few second later emerges wearing a burqa and hurries off.

Farida

(to herself)

So that's your trick you dirty bastard.

She follows him through the narrow streets to the house of Amira, his lover. Farida is beside herself with anger.

Ext. Field - Day - Continuous

Farida arrives at a field and calls to a young man plowing with an ox.

Farida

Good day Safwan!

Safwan (22) stops his work and comes towards Farida with the ox.

Safwan

Hello Farida. How are you?

Farida

How is your sister Amira? I suppose her life has completely changed since she lost her husband in battle.

Safwan

Yes, she must look after her children. I help her as much as I can, but she lives a harsh life.

Farida

I feel sorry for her. But I wonder if what I heard this morning is true...

Safwan

What is that?

Farida

A friend has told me she is receiving men...

The eyes of Safwan grow large with anger.

Safwan

Who is this friend of yours? Who are you to tell me this? Amira is a righteous woman!

Farida

I am sorry, I guess I should not have told you. But you should check on her. I'm sorry, please have a nice day...

Farida leaves. Safwan watches her go, shaking his head in doubt and disgust.

Ext. Seville streets - Day

Safwan has left his work in the fields and carries a basket of potatoes and tomatoes to his sister Amira. He arrives at her home and knocks at the door. She answers.

Int. Amira's house - Day - Continuous

Safwan puts the basket of vegetables on the table. He kisses the children, playing on the floor. He turns to Amira.

Safwan

You look happier these days. Has something happened?

Amira

No... No there is nothing. The kids are fine. And you care for us so well (kissing him on the cheek.)

Safwan

(Discreetly looking around the apartment for clues. He finds none.)

Well then, I'm off now. If I didn't have the cows and horses to look after I'd come and live with you.

Amira

Don't worry about me. I'm fine.

Safwan kisses his sister goodbye and leaves.

Ext. La Giralda square - Dusk

Safwan walks through the square and hears the sunset call to prayer from la Giralda mosque. He decides to stop in.

Int. Mosque - Day - Continuous

The main floor of the mosque is filled with men quietly and amiably chatting. Women are in another section, and their soft laughter can be heard from the entrance. Safwan joins the men, and the prayer begins. After prayer, he approaches Khalid (40s) a stern looking man with a beard but no mustache. He wears an immaculate grey robe.

Safwan

Assalam Alaikom.

Khalid

Walaikom Assalam.

Safwan

I would like you to advise me on the matter of sharia.

Khalid

Go ahead.

Safwan

If a woman has a lover and they are not married, and one of her family members finds out, what should he do?

Khalid

She should be stoned, and her lover beaten.

Safwan

You mean their death in such circumstances is not a crime and would not offend God?

Khalid

No. Such a death would protect the morality of society and God would bless it.

Safwan looks up to the ceiling, pondering, and Khalid takes his leave.

Int. Ahmad's house - Day

Farida prepares herself and her daughter to attend the musical performance at the palace. Ahmad is observing his wife.

Ahmad

And what about the three boys, aren't they going?

Son

We're not interested in music.

Farida and her daughter leave the house. Ahmad leaves after her with his bag and burqa.

Ext. Amira's house - Night

Safwan waits outside of his sister Amira's home, high up in a tree. Soon a figure in a burqa (Ahmad) knocks at the door and enters when Amira answers. Safwan jumps down from the tree and hides near the window, listening to voices inside.

Ahmad

My wife has gone to the concert at the palace.

Amira

I'm so glad you came to me...

Int. Amira's house - Night - Continuous

Safwan opens the front door quietly and sneaks into the house. He can see the lovers undressing by lamp light in the bedroom. They sink to the bed passionately embracing.

Safwan strikes. He pulls a knife from his belt and stabs Ahmad in the back. Amira, on her back, sees his figure as he towers over her, stabbing her lover, terror in her eyes, she screams and faints from fear.

Beautiful music from the palace floats through the violent evening.

Int. Caliphs palace garden - Night

Hundreds of people gather in the palace garden, listening to the concert. Strings of lights and candles and lamps light up the evening, the walls are draped with lush curtains and shear silks billow in the slight breeze. The musicians are on stage in the center, playing a song called "Lamma bada yatathanna", a well-known musical. Dancers take to the floor.

Farida is enjoying herself. Um and Abu Omar sit on a sofa, proudly watching as their son Omar plays his rebab.

Averroes sits among friends and students. His daughter Rabab admires him and taps her father's elbow.

Rabab

Omar is brilliant, isn't he?

Averroes

Indeed, he is. He puts so much feeling into his playing. (smirking with some self-satisfaction) they took my remarks to heart.

The musical ends.

Int. Ahmad's house - Night

Farida and her daughter arrive home. The boys are sleeping but the father is not home. Farida's anger grows.

Farida

(to her daughter) go to bed.

Farida turns and departs out the front door.

Ext. Amira's house - Night - Continuous

Farida knocks and Amira opens the door fearfully, tears streaking her face.

Farida

Where is my husband, you bitch?

She pushes Amira and enters the house. The kids are sleeping and there is no one.

Farida attacks Amira and pulls at her hair.

Farida

Where is my husband? I know he has been visiting you. Where is he?

Amira explodes into tears and begins babbling incoherently.

Amira

I don't know! Leave me alone!

Int. Ahmad's house - Night - Continuous

Farida sits in her home, waiting for her husband till the first rays of light. He does not return.

Ext. Seville security post - Day

Early morning, Farida goes to the security officers, and they listen as she describes the situation.

Farida

(in tears)

... I don't understand, we have been married for 23 years...

Int. Amira's house - Day

Security officers arrest Amira.

Ext. Field - Day

Officers arrest Safwan as he plows his field.

Ext. River - Day

Officers pull Ahmad's mangled body out of the river.

Int. Prison - Day

Averroes visits Safwan and Amira in jail and speaks with them quietly.

Ext. Seville streets - Day

Sarah's wagon, driven by Robert, drives through the city gates and through the streets to la Giralda square. Passersby recognize Sarah and call out to welcome her. She guides Robert to her home.

Sarah

Turn right at the edge of the square, Robert.

Robert

You are very popular here.

An old couple selling vegetables waves at Sarah as she passes.

Sarah

Wonderful people. My true home.

Ext. Sarah's residence - Day

The wagon drives into a large house with a beautiful garden courtyard. Dozens of children run out to welcome Sarah, kissing and hugging her.

Robert

(surprised)

Who are these children?

Sarah

I run an orphanage. With the wars so many children are losing their families. I employ some of the widows and two men to look after them.

Robert

I am speechless... You are a great lady, a great soul.

The five men and women of the orphanage come out to greet Sarah.

Sarah

Any new children?

Widow I

We have recently taken in two little boys. They were brought by the city guards. Their father died two years ago in the siege of Lisbon. Their mother and their uncle have been arrested for adultery and murder. Their trial will take place this afternoon.

Sarah

Such a sad story! I trust that the new caliph has retained Averroes as judge of the city?

Man I

Yes. Thankfully he holds the keys to our city. The caliph Abu Yusuf accompanied the body of his father to Marrakesh.

Sarah

Then we need not worry. A just trial will be held.

Robert

Who is this Averroes you speak of with such high respect?

Sarah

For me he is the wisest man on earth. The kindest soul you can ever meet.

Robert

I would like to attend the trial. Will it be open to the public?

Sarah

Yes, I think you should go. I am exhausted so I will stay home. You can come inside and wash up.

They enter Sarah's home-turned-orphanage surrounded by the children.

Int. Caliphs palace amphitheater - Day

The midday calls to prayer floats through the streets and Robert, fresh in his best English traveling clothes, a stranger in a strange land, arrives in the palace amphitheater. Students and spectators enter and take their seats. They greet the newcomer shyly.

A panel of magistrates, one of them Abu Utaiba (50s) enters and sits near the center. Averroes enters and makes his way to the center of the amphitheater, pleasantly greeting all he passes. Imam Khalid, Farida and the brother of Ahmad sit in the front row.

Finally, a signal is given, and all activity stops. The three accused, Safwan, Amira, and Khalid, are led by guards into the center. Averroes opens the trial.

Averroes

Bismillah al Rahman al Raheem. In the name of God, the most gracious, the most compassionate. We are gathered today to seek justice in the murder of Ahmad ben Hammoud.

The three accused are brought before Averroes.

Averroes

Safwan Elmaghrabi and Amira Elmaghrabi, brother and sister, are accused of committing this crime.

Amira weeps and Safwan remains dispassionately aloof.

Averroes

And the imam Khalid Shaaban is accused of incitement to murder.

Khalid stands defiant, his eyes closed.

Averroes

The widow the brother of the murdered man has asked us to seek justice. They shall speak first and when they are done, I shall pose my questions. We will then hear from the committee of judges and finally I will give my final judgment. I call Farida to the stand. What are your accusations?

Farida steps up and swears upon the Quran.

Farida

I swear to God I will say nothing but the truth. One week ago, I discovered my husband, Ahmad, was visiting the widow Amira in her home by day. I was trying to figure out how to confront him when three nights ago I attended the musical at the palace with my daughter. When I returned home my husband was not there. I reported his absence to the city guards, and they pulled his body from the river, where Safwan threw it. I accuse Amira and Safwan Elmaghrabi of killing my husband and I would like to see them punished by death for their crime.

Averroes

We have heard your accusation. I call Amira Elmaghrabi to the stand.

Amira approaches, vulnerable but clear eyed. She has decided to tell the truth as seen by her heart.

Amira

My husband fought and died in Lisbon for our way of life. I loved him, and I always will. But as time has passed, I have realized I have other... I am alone in this world and I am... Young...

Averroes listens intently. The compassion in his eyes gives her courage to continue.

Amira

I have physical needs, the needs of a woman of child-bearing age. My husband's absence has left me with no way to fulfill them. One day I met Ahmad in the street, and he said that my husband was one of the best soldiers in Andalusia. He said he would like to help me look after my children. Later he knocked at my door, his arms full of gifts for the little ones and I could not refuse his generosity. That is when it began. I needed his attention and kindness, I felt safe when he was there. (She weeps and has difficulty continuing.)

Averroes nods, patiently waiting for her to continue. She dries her tears and goes on with determination.

Amira

That horrible night, he knocked on my door. I was overwhelmed with happiness to see him. He came in and we let our passion consume us. And then, I saw this angry silhouette. The next thing I remember, I woke up to the fierce pounding on the door. It was Farida, she attacked me, screaming about her husband. I told her I didn't know... And in the morning the guards arrested me...

Amira sits. Silence fills the courtroom.

Averroes

Safwan.

Safwan

When Farida told me my sister Amira was receiving men secretly, I went mad. I consulted imam Khalid to find out the rules for dealing with adulterers, and he confirmed what I had already heard: that we should rid society of their menace. So, I did my duty: I waited for Ahmad to appear, I confirmed with my eyes that they were engaged in lascivious acts, and I stabbed him.

Averroes listens with the same compassion he showed Amira.

Safwan

But I was weak: I could not kill my sister. So, I will wait for judgment to be passed upon her by your court, and I believe you will come to the same conclusion I did. I confess everything because I did what was right and there is no point in denying my actions.

Averroes nods and Safwan takes his seat.

Averroes

Imam Khalid.

Khalid

Safwan approached me after the sunset prayer and asked me general questions about sharia. I answered him with my knowledge, but I certainly had no clue that he was speaking of a personal affair. Maybe if I had known, I would have spoken with more caution.

Averroes

Farida. Is it true that you looked out Safwan in the fields and told him about his sister's activities?

Farida

(nervous)

Yes.

Averroes

And have you already spoken to your husband about his affair with Amira?

Farida

No.

Averroes

Perhaps you should have done so instead of getting revenge by way of Safwan.

Averroes turns to the hall.

Averroes

You all claim you admire the life of your prophet, but when it comes to your daily lives you act in the name of your egos. It's clear that in times of war many men are killed, and many young women are widowed. We have seen cities where the number of women is twice that of men! And for this reason, we allow men to have more than one wife.

He turns to Farida.

Averroes

You chose not to discuss the matter with your husband. You chose to take your revenge on him instead. And in doing so you brought two vulnerable souls into a family matter.

Farida

(crying, eyes cast downwards)

I did not imagine that Safwan would go so far as to kill him... I really am sorry. I am a bad woman.

Farida can no longer look at Averroes.

Averroes

Amira, had you ever discussed marriage with Ahmad?

Amira

Of course, we wanted to marry. He already had Farida, and he said he would speak to her when he found the right time. The chemistry between us was right, we had such passion and laughter, and I believe he was serious about marrying me in the future.

Averroes

Safwan, after hearing these details, do you regret what you have done?

Safwan

(head held high)

No. This is the honor of my family. I cannot have my
nephews growing up in a whorehouse.

Averroes

(angrily)

The honor of a family, young man, is not found
between the legs of a woman! Honor is in
understanding, in empathy, in one's capacity to love,
in tolerance and in forgiving.

Another magistrate, Abu Utaiba stands to object.

Abu Utaiba

I would like to add my voice. Safwan has taken justice
into his own hands. The law makes it clear that the
killer must be killed.

Averroes

Magistrate Abu Utaiba, you, like Imam Khalid, studied
at the al Azhar Mosque so it does not surprise me to
hear you say this. However, what I find strange is that
your teachings tell us that Safwan should be a hero
for avenging the honor of his family, and yet you are
saying he must be killed.

Averroes turns to Safwan.

Averroes

How shall we explain this, young man. Two men, same religious school. And yet one encouraged you to kill in cold blood, and the other wants you to be killed. I wonder what makes them hate life so? Why do they want to be surrounded by dead people?

Magistrate Abu Utaiba

(angrily protests)

Both of them should be killed! He and his sister. That is what the sharia says.

Khalid

Yes, our duty is to protect society from sinners.

Averroes

No. This is not going to happen. Surely this verse is speaking about people like you: "the true danger to society is he who buys amusement of speech to mislead others from the way of god without knowledge and who takes it in ridicule. "

70

Robert is listening intently. Another magistrate joins the debate.

Magistrate

But Averroes, Amira is a sinner, and she should get her punishment. However, if you find Safwan to be the guilty one, he should be killed. A crime has been committed and someone should face death.

Averroes

What is it with all of you and the death penalty? When did the verb repent disappear? Have you forgotten that Moses killed an Egyptian man before God accepted his repentance and made him messenger and prophet?

A man from the audience, Ahmad's brother, cries out.

Ahmad's brother

And what of the blood of my brother? Has it spilled so cheaply?

Averroes

I demand calm before you hear the verdict. We will pause for deliberation.

Averroes leaves center stage. The audience waits
patiently. A few minutes later Averroes returns, a
document in hand.

Averroes takes the center to pass the verdict.

Averroes

The loss of the life of Ahmad ben Hammoud is sad for
our community. After hearing the witnesses, the
accusers and the accused, I have come to see clearly
that four people were involved directly and indirectly
in the crime. Three of them acted in a way that led to
the death of Ahmad: Khalid with his ignorance, Farida
with her jealousy, and Safwan with his arrogance. The
only person who acted out of truth and love is Amira.

Surprised murmurs in the courtroom.

Averroes

The high court of Andalusia rules the following: Imam
Khalid is stripped of his license as a Muslim scholar,
he will no longer be an Imam. His brand of extremism
is a real danger to society so he will remain under
house arrest until further decision from the caliph.

Farida ben Hammoud has been found guilty of inciting murder. She takes her punishment with her to her grave: she is now a widow like Amira, and we shall see how she copes without a partner by her side. Married or not, no one owns another person. If only she had understood beforehand that love should always dominate the heart and that our tongues were given to us by God so as to speak in a manner of understanding and love.

Safwan Elmaghrabi is found guilty in the killing of Ahmad ben Hammoud. He will therefore get a life sentence in jail. He shows no signs of regret. He deliberately consulted Khalid because that was the message he wanted to hear. He could have come to me, but he chose extremism instead of a moderated approach. Let this be a lesson for all of us. He can, however, if he decides, choose a more moderate path and reduce his sentence.

Amira Elmaghrabi is innocent, the victim of hate and intolerance.

The belongings of Safwan Elmaghrabi will be transferred to Ahmad's children and his brother as recompense. The palace will give Amira money to look after her two children and to relocate to another city if she likes. Her life here in Seville will likely be unbearable after the trial. We offer her this choice so that she can have an opportunity to start anew, and we wish her brighter days after the devastating loss of not one, but two loved ones.

Averroes

In the name of the high court of Andalusia, I declare this case closed.

The trial ends.

A protest rises from some corners of the amphitheater, and guards come in to move people out.

Int. Sarah's house - Day

Robert and Sarah are sitting casually in her salon and eating fruits.

Robert

I must admit, I am impressed by this man, Averroes. There is such a difference between him and our inquisitors.

Sarah

Oh, and you haven't yet seen the best of him. If he was Jewish, I would say he is the messiah!

Robert

I would love to get to know such a man.

Sarah

I will introduce you to him.

Int. Caliphs palace lecture hall - Night

Averroes is circulating among his many students, who are reading, studying and playing music. He approaches Omar and Yazeed who are practicing music and picks up his oud. He shows them some techniques and they take notes. Rabab and David are studying nearby. A servant enters.

Servant

Sarah Abraham of Barchenona has come with a friend to see you.

Averroes

Please let them in, she will enjoy the music.

He rises to greet them. Sarah and Averroes embrace as old friends.

Averroes

What a long time it has been, dear Sarah.

Sarah

I have brought Robert of St. Albans to meet you. He comes from England.

Averroes

(to Robert)

Wonderful to meet you, Robert. Welcome to Andalusia. We have with us a young student from England.

(pointing toward David)

His name is David, a fitting name because he is as great as king David! He has a brilliant mind and an open heart.

Sarah

I was always impressed by what the prophet Muhammad said about David's prayer. What was it again?

Averroes

Oh yes, Muhammad said that the most beloved prayer to God was David's prayer. He had a great voice, and he played great music.

Sarah

Do you have any singers here?

Averroes

We have Aisha and Omar. They both have beautiful voices.

Sarah

(to Omar)

Do you know the old Jewish song (hums "I will dance like David danced, a traditional song.)

Omar smiles and joins her in the song.

Omar

It's one of my favorites!

Sarah

Play the music! And let us dance like David danced!

The musicians begin to play, and Sarah grabs Averroes' hands and they dance.

Robert

(to David)

This is unbelievable. A paradise. What a difference from the barbaric world we live in!

Sarah grabs Robert and David's hands and pulls them into the dance. The four laugh as they move to the music.

Finally, the music stops, and Averroes comes to Robert's side, laughing and wiping his brow.

Robert

I have so many questions for you after your performance in court. Could you give me a bit of your time so we can discuss it one-on-one?

Averroes

Are you an early riser? The best time to have a long conversation is just after morning prayer in the palace garden. You can meet me there at sunrise.

Robert

I'll be there.

Rabab

(to Omar)

You were great tonight as usual. I am a fan of your talent. And your voice.

Omar

(beaming) thank you.

Averroes and Sarah exchange a look as they notice the shy flirtation between Rabab and Omar.

Ext. Caliphs palace garden - Sunrise

Averroes, dressed in white, prays at sunrise in the gardens. Robert arrives and takes in the beauty of the scene, water pouring from a fountain and the scent of jasmine teasing his nose. He sits down on a patch of grass not far from Averroes.

Averroes finishes his prayer and joins Robert.

Averroes

Good morning, Englishman! We can go inside if you like.

Robert

No. It is wonderful here.

Averroes

I'm looking forward to hearing your story.

From afar we see Robert tells Averroes about his experience in tours, Robert breaking down and Averroes comforting him.

Averroes

I do understand your frustration and anger toward the church. I believe it is time to awaken the people and bring about a revolution inside your religious teachings. The pope may claim to be teaching Jesus words, but that doesn't mean he actually is.

Robert

I know that if Jesus was among us now, he wouldn't allow such cruelty. Those who claim to follow him are the most dangerous beings on earth. I feel I should do something about them, but I am not an intellectual. I know nothing of religion in general, I know very little about Judaism or Islam.

Averroes

You are speaking as if these three beliefs were different from each other while they are not: they are just an evolution of human faith in God, that is all.

Robert

but you and the Jews believe in one God the Almighty, the creator of everything and each of us is responsible for his actions. We believe that Jesus died on the cross to erase our sins.

Averroes

And what are your heart and mind telling you? Think logically and rationally about things. If Jesus died to save humanity, then why all the death, illness, wars, misery around us? And if you believe God is the creator of everything and always just, then why would he allow the pope or a savage king to massacre his people or wage war, and then forgive him just because they say they love Jesus. This is nonsense. You must believe that you and only you are responsible for your own actions and deeds. God can forgive what's between you and him, but he certainly can't forgive whatever harm you do me. If I don't forgive you myself, God can't tell me to forget about it if I am demanding justice. What goes around comes around. You will pay for the bad you do, either here in this life or in the eternal one.

Robert is thinking, and then he laughs.

Robert

81

You know what I've never understood? Our leaders tell us there's one God, and then they tell us there are three! Don't they see the contradiction?

Averroes

The trinity was just an invention by Byzantium that fit in better with the pagan beliefs. But God is one and only, he has no wives, no sons, he is the light of heaven and earth. So, Jesus was the product of the holy spirit trapped in a human body, not God himself.

Robert

I'm confused because there are good teachings in the bibles we have.

Averroes

Yes of course there are wonderful things!

Robert

I don't know. I just hate what the pope is doing with the church. I will think about all that you said. (a beat) I admire you too much to hide anything from you, and in matter of total respect I want to tell you frankly that I am here on a mission. The king of

England sent me to see how things are going in Andalusia after the death of caliph Abu Yaqub. King Henry II considers Andalusia a friend and we are worried about the inquisition and the growing power of the Castilians and the Portuguese. What can you tell me about the new caliph?

Averroes

He is young and strong; he has the charisma to lead. But at the intellectual level he has a lot to learn. So, nothing much has changed; the son is like the father. As for harmonious coexistence, I can assure you that for as long as I live, Andalusia's heart will remain open to all people who run away from persecution in Europe and other places.

Int. Beaumont palace - Day

Caption: 1185 AD

Robert has returned to king Henry II with his reports on Andalusia.

Robert

Andalusia is heaven on earth. They have a genius called Averroes, a very wise man. They value every moment of their time. It's indeed in our favor if they control all of Iberia.

Henry II

I wish I could visit. Is it more beautiful than
Jerusalem?

Robert

Yes, because holy land has become a center of war
with the pope's crusade.

Henry II

Averroes. I have heard of him from our savants. Do
you think he could translate the pages of our book?
Our scholars have not made a breakthrough now for
months.

Robert

I'm sure he can find a way. I'll gladly bring a copy to
him.

Henry II

Do it and keep me informed on how things progress.

Ext. Southern Spain - Day

Robert and his sister Camilla ride their horses south
to Andalusia.

Int. Seville palace - Day

Rabab and Averroes in the palace. Rabab has two astrolabes in her hands.

Rabab

I am very fond of physics, mathematics and astronomy. I would like to specialize in them, if I have your blessing.

Averroes

You know I respect freedom of choice. Go ahead and show me if you are able to surpass Maryam, who made those brilliant devices you hold in your hands. I have only one worry.

Rabab

worry about what?

Averroes

(smiling)

I am worried about how a future scientist can build a harmonious relationship with a talented musician.

Rabab blushes and smiles shyly.

Averroes

Do you think I haven't noticed the passion you have for each other? Come my little child, I only want to see you happy.

He hugs his daughter.

Averroes

I know where there is true love there will be happiness. And there, numbers and spheres can easily become the musical notes of a beautiful symphony.

Ext. Riverside - Day

On a hot day on the quiet riverbank, Abu Omar is laying in the sun masturbating. He climaxes, but soon afterward he cries with loneliness and the absurdity he feels.

Eventually he calms down and jumps in the river to wash. He gets out and dries off, puts his clothes back on.

Up the river some bushes rustle: someone has been watching him.

Int. Caliphs palace observatory - Night

Averroes is sitting in the audience of an astronomy and physics lecture with his closest students, among others. Among the students is Hussein (30).

Yazeed

I brought with me today some Ptolemy handy tables. I hope they are useful to make precise calculations about the positions of the planets, especially the moon and the sun.

Averroes purses his lips in disagreement. Rabab notices.

Rabab

I don't think it's a good idea. My father doesn't agree at all with Ptolemy about astronomy.

Yazeed

(winking at Averroes)

I don't think that Ptolemy and his almagest are the problem as much as the scientist who translated them into Arabic.

David

You mean Avicenna!

Hussein rolls his eyes and writes something in his notebook.

Averroes

(laughing)

Yazeed you are a little devil, you know me very well, don't you? By the way Ben Isaac was the translator of Ptolemy to Arabic. Avicenna just perfected the translation.

Hussein sees the affection of Averroes to Yazeed and feels something approaching jealousy.

A servant interrupts.

Servant

Robert of England has returned, sir.

Averroes

Alright. I'll be with him in a moment. (turning to students) each one of you can work on the topic he desires tonight, but don't forget we will focus on the moon study in the coming month; therefore, you should sacrifice some time to revise my theory on the subject.

Int. Caliphs palace - Night

Robert and Camilla are sitting in the main hall of the palace. Averroes enters and shakes their hands.

Averroes

We have a visitor. A very beautiful young lady!

Robert

Yes, this is my sister Camilla. She is new here. (observing his sister) we don't have all of this luxury in England.

Averroes

Welcome to your city Camilla. I am sure you will enjoy your time here.

Robert

She will live here and study with your students. She is a few years younger than David, and I hope they will look after each other, since they come from the same land.

Averroes

I am sure she will do well. I can read intelligence in her eyes. (making fun of himself) I have experience in spotting these things.

Robert

She will stay at Sarah's house.

Averroes

She can begin attending the classes she wants tomorrow.

Robert

I hope to see you after the morning prayer if you are free to talk.

Averroes

Yes, you must tell me news from England.

Robert turns to leave.

Robert

Very good. Assalam Alaikom.

Averroes

Peace be upon you too.

Robert and Camilla leave, Averroes rejoins his class.

Ext. Caliphs palace garden - Sunrise

At the first rays of the sun, Averroes and Robert walk in the gardens. Robert hands Averroes the white book from Solomon's temple.

Averroes

What is this?

Robert

I found this book at Solomon's temple in Jerusalem. Do you recognize the language?

Averroes

(thumbing through the book, his eyes glowing with curiosity)

I'm not sure, but it looks like an Amorite language.

Robert

Can you read anything? The title?

Averroes

I don't know the script. I may have a book which contains translations from Amorite to Arabic or Hebrew, and we can use them to decipher it. It will take time... We don't have any experts in the Amorite languages.

Robert

There's no hurry.

Averroes

I can't promise anything. But we will try.

Robert

I've made up my mind.

Averroes

About what?

Robert

I want to convert officially to Islam.

Averroes

(surprised)

What do you mean by officially? I told you before that if you believe in God, it's enough. Why do you want to categorize yourself?

Robert

No, it's not enough. I need an official certificate that I am a Muslim.

Averroes

(annoyed)

What for? Do you want to marry a Muslim woman?

Robert

I want to return to Jerusalem.

Averroes is stunned.

Robert

I want to fight in the Muslim army against the
crusaders.

Averroes

(angry and disappointed)

I understand your rage against the church, but do you
think the Muslim warriors of Egypt and the levant are
angels? Oh, my son, you are mistaken. There is a
dangerous extremism growing like cancer and in
their war with the crusaders... Well, the best I can say
is they are the lesser of two evils. So don't fool
yourself by thinking that if Muslims took back control
of Jerusalem things would get back to happy old days.
Those who are fighting each other believe in a
bloodthirsty god. They have forgotten my god and
yours, the merciful and graceful one.

Robert

I fought on the side of the crusaders, and I feel
betrayed and misled by the church. I want to repay
the debt and fight for the least evil side, if that is what
you call it.

Averroes

Then why don't you join our army here, and defend the lifestyle and civilization we have created in Andalusia? Here we defend, we never attack.

Robert

My debt is in Jerusalem, and that is where I need to repay it. And there's another thing...

Averroes

Yes?

Robert

I believe the Christian armies attacking you from the north are gaining morale since Jerusalem fell to the church.

Averroes

If you are convinced that what you are going to do is right, then I can't convince you otherwise. For me, God calls for peace, not for war unless we are defending ourselves.

Robert

So, will you sign this certificate?

Averroes

I don't do such procedures myself. But you can go to the mosque and ask the imam to officiate your conversion from Christianity to Islam.

Int. Mosque - Day

Robert stands in front of the imam, who recites from the Quran. Robert repeats.

Robert

I witness that there is only one God and Muhammad is his messenger.

The imam hands him a signed certificate.

Imam

You are now one of us. Welcome to the Islamic faith.

Int. Palace lecture hall - Night

Averroes is giving a lecture. A servant interrupts.

Servant

A messenger from Marrakesh sir.

Averroes leaves his lecture and walks into the hallway.

Int. Hallway - Night – Continuous

Averroes greets the messenger.

Messenger

Assalam Alaikum.

Averroes

Walaykum Assalam.

Messenger

The health of our master Ibn Tufail is deteriorating, and he wishes to see you. In respect to all of his achievements, the caliph vowed to make this happen.

Averroes

He was my teacher. Of course, I must see him. I will travel tomorrow morning.

Ext. Palace gates - Day

Averroes and Robert are saying goodbye to their loved ones at the palace gates. Averroes is in a wagon, surrounded by guards. Robert dressed in Almohad armor, astride a horse. Robert hugs his sister Camilla. David stands by her side.

Robert

You are in the safest place on earth, dear sister. You will learn wonderful things here. And you are already good friends with David, I see...

Camilla

(tearfully)

I don't understand why you must go to such a horrible place. Life here is peaceful and we are together.

Robert

I am going for the sake of the peace you are living in here. If we are to keep this place safe, the church must be defeated over there. Pray for me sister, I will not return before I help deliver the holy land to its rightful keepers.

Yazeed arrives breathless carrying his bag with him.

Averroes

What is this?

Yazeed

I want to be your travel companion.

Averroes

Well, that would be great. It's a long journey and it will be wonderful to have a travel companion.

Yazeed

Great! How can I miss the chance to meet the great novelist who wrote "Hay Ben Yaqzan"?

Averroes

And I thought you were coming for my company.

Rabab

Take care. Have a safe journey.

Averroes points to Alpetragius (50), a fellow scholar.

Averroes

I leave my classes in the hands of Alpetragius, (turning to rabab) and I trust you to help him to keep things in order.

Rabab nods her head in agreement.

David

Have a safe journey. Don't worry about Camilla, she'll be fine. (He puts his hands on her shoulder.)

Robert hugs his sister one last time. Averroes wagon surrounded by a few guards, leaves, and Robert rides beside him.

Ext. Tangiers port - Day

Averroes, Yazeed, and Robert debark a luxurious boat into the crowded port city of Tangiers. People from all over the mediterranean world circulate in the crowd, unloading ships and selling goods. There are fishermen, women, children, and chaos.

Robert

Now I turn towards the holy land.

Averroes

I hope you achieve your dreams. Once you arrive in the lands of Egypt, you will be at the heart of the Ayyubid kingdom. You already have a reputation there as a great warrior, so show them your certificate and ask to join their army.

Robert waves goodbye and rides his horse east.

Ext. Desert road - Day

Averroes and Yazeed ride in their wagon on the road to Marrakesh.

Averroes

(to Yazeed)

I'm glad you came with me. Time passes quickly when you are by my side.

Yazeed

I am lucky to have you as a teacher and friend. And I'm excited to meet the teacher of my teacher!

Averroes

Abu Bakr Ibn Tufail summoned me one day and told me that he had heard the caliph complaining about the disjointedness of Aristotle's mode of expression -- or that of the translators -- and the resultant obscurity of his intentions. He said that if someone took on these books and summarized them and clarified their aims after first thoroughly understanding them himself, people would have an easier time comprehending them.

"If you have the energy, " he told me, "You do it. I'm confident you can, because I know what a good mind and devoted character you have, and how dedicated you are to the art. "

(to Yazeed) You must understand that it was his old age, the worries of his office and his commitment to other tasks kept him from doing it himself.

Yazeed

That's why you dedicated most of your time recently to reconcile between Greek philosophy and Islam.

Averroes

It's always important to collect the best knowledge and ideas that we have in the present and the past to build a solid base for the future. I want my work to be like honey made by bees from many different flowers.

Yazeed

After I read your commentaries, I had the impression that you agree with Plato more than Aristotle.

Averroes

Yes. True. Aristotle went too far in his thoughts about the divine, while Plato showed in his thinking complete trust in our creator. Plato said, "we ought to fly away from earth to heaven as quickly as we can; and to fly away is to become like god, as far as this is possible; and to become like him is to become holy, just, and wise. "

On the other hand, Aristotle held some negative views about God. He said "if some animals are good at hunting and others are suitable for hunting, then the gods must clearly smile on hunting. " How would you explain that? God is playing a game with all of his creatures? That does not seem very godlike!

I agree with him on many other points such as the eternity of the universe, but globally I am more impressed by his scientific work than his philosophical and social ideas. Therefor I speak of him the same way he spoke of Plato: Aristotle is dear to me, but dearer still is the truth.

Ext. Marrakesh - Day

Averroes and Yazeed arrive in Marrakesh. As they walk through the narrow streets, news of Averroes arrival spreads and doors open as if by intuition. People come out onto the streets to greet him. Guards bow in respect.

Int. Ibn Tufail's room - Day - Continuous

Sunlight speckles the dark room where Ibn Tufail lays in bed coughing. His eyes brighten in happiness as Averroes enters the room. He smiles as widely as he can in his weakened state. The two wise men hug and tears of joy stream down their faces.

Averroes

I have come to be with my wise old teacher.

Ibn Tufail

My game is over. 80 years is enough, isn't it?

Averroes

There is never enough time for a visionary such as you.

Ibn Tufail

I have done my bit, given what I can give. Now I hope to hear some good news from you. Tell me of your latest writings and studies. Tell me about your students and of Andalusia. Tell me of this paradise I yearn for...

Averroes

I am fulfilling your wishes. I am commenting on all the available books of Plato and Aristotle, and I have already finished many of them. (motioning to Yazeed) I would like to introduce you to my dear student, Yazeed. As you see, he is still young and strong, he is the future of Andalusia.

Yazeed

It is a privilege to meet you, sir. I find your novel "Hay Ben Yaqzan" to be perfect. I enjoyed every word. And I believe that it influenced my teacher as well, especially his most recent book the incoherence of the incoherence. He writes that one should

103

contemplate the nature of everything in its purity, since what is added is an obstacle to its knowledge.

Averroes laughs.

Averroes

(quoting his own work) Contemplate therefore the soul in its abstraction or rather let him who makes this abstraction contemplate himself in this state and he will know that he is immortal when he will see in himself the purity of the intellect, for he will see his intellect contemplate nothing sensible, nothing mortal, but apprehending the eternal through the eternal.

The two older men smile appreciatively at Yazeed.

Averroes

You see what a sharp analytical mind he has.

Yazeed, slightly embarrassed, reaches into his satchel and pulls out the book given to Averroes by Robert. Averroes is pleasantly surprised to see the book in his students' hands.

Yazeed

Perhaps you could help us. We received this book from Jerusalem, but we have yet to find a key to translate it.

The old man takes the book in his withered hands, treating it as a precious object. He Leafs through the pages.

Ibn Tufail

Yes, it appears to be in one of the Amorite languages... I remember years ago meeting a Christian monk from Baghdad who was searching for original versions of the bible. He was living in a monastery near Cordoba... (pointing to his desk) Yazeed, hand me that book, I'll give you his name...

Yazeed retrieves the book. Ibn Tufail hands shake as he turns the pages.

Ibn Tufail

How about medicine? How are the experiments in body dissection?

Averroes

I am still fighting to allow more dissections, as you know, the religious restrictions are blocking the way.

Ibn Tufail

(finding the name) Ah here it is!

Int. Cairo palace - Day

Robert enters the palace of the Ayyubids, accompanied by two guards.

Guard I

Your transfer to the first army couldn't be easier, you are fortunate because princess Sitt al-sham Zumurrud is in Cairo for a few days. She wants to see you.

They lead him towards a large door.

Int. Cairo palace study - Day

The guard and Robert enter a large study. A young woman, princess Alia (22) is deep in concentration, writing something. She is startled by the two arrivals.

Guard I

Assalam Alaikom lady Alia, we are sorry for disturbing you, but your mother the princess said she wants to meet us here.

Alia

(shyly)

Walaikum Assalam. I am sorry I did not know of the arrangement.

She looks Robert straight in the eye, then leaves the room through a small door.

Princes Zumurrud (45), a tall, elegant woman with the green eyes of her Kurdish ancestors, enters the room.

Zumurrud

Peace be upon you.

Robert and the two guards bow.

Robert

Walaikum Assalam, princess Zumurrud.

Zumurrud

Will you introduce us?

Guard

This is Robert of St. Albans a former templar from England. He used to fight with the crusaders, but he has now converted to Islam, and he is eager to join our army.

Zumurrud

Tell me Robert, why is this rare change in your
beliefs?

Robert

Life in Europe under the church is a nightmare. They
don't care about science, knowledge, wisdom, or
justice. They only believe in their own dogmatic faith,
and they worship power and wealth. I had the
privilege to stay a few weeks in Andalusia where I
met the savant of all savants, the wisest man on earth,
Averroes. And after talking to him I decided to
convert to Islam in order to fight against the church.

Zumurrud

you are a lucky man. I am impressed by his work, he's
such a genius. I dream of meeting him face to face.
Tell me, what does he look like?

Robert

He is in his early 60s, his face shines like the moon,
surrounded by white and grey hair and a soft beard.
His eyes are blue. His face looks as if it has been
carefully painted by a great artist... He is wonderful
from inside and out.

Zumurrud

Have mercy! This description will tempt me to pay a visit to the west! (a beat) and what of this certificate?

Robert hands her the paper which declares his conversion to Islam. Zumurrud examines it, considering it carefully. Finally, she looks up.

Zumurrud

I am leaving for Damascus in two days. You are welcome to join us on the trip. I will introduce you to my brother Saladin upon arrival.

Robert bows down.

Robert

Thank you, princess.

Int. Rabat palace- Day

Averroes and Abu Yusuf speak.

Averroes

How are things with the rebels?

Caliph

The Moravids are a thorn in the side of our kingdom. We must be rid of their nuisance as soon as possible so I can return to Europe to carry out justice in the name of my father.

Averroes

I wish you could just trust in the strength of your defenses and forget about wars for a while.

Caliph

You live in your imaginary world, my friend. In this world, if you don't strike first, they will come and attack you.

Averroes

Defend your land but do not initiate attacks.

Caliph

Don't annoy me with your exaggerated wisdom now. Come to the hammam and massage my back. I heard from my father that you are a good physician.

Averroes

Oh, here we go again.

Int. Hammam - Day

Averroes and Abu Yusuf, enter the palace hammam, towels around their waists. The room is tiled and luxurious, with light filtering in through the steam.

Caliph

I must admit you have a beautiful daughter.

Averroes

And your wife is a beautiful woman too.

A servant interrupts.

Servant

Sad news from Marrakesh, Ibn Tufail has left us.

Averroes

(In sadness, excusing himself to Abu Yusuf)

I must return, I gave him my word to bury him.

The caliph nods.

Ext. Marrakesh cemetery - Day

Averroes and Yazeed bury Ibn Tufail's body
according to Islamic tradition as interpreted by
Averroes. It is a humble, simple ceremony. The body's
head faces mecca. The body, beneath a white shroud,
is naked. Averroes piles stones and then sand upon
the body.

Ext. Road - Day

The caravan from Cairo travels on the road to Damascus. Calvary and guards stretch as far as the eye can see. A wagon carries Zumurrud and Alia, and Robert rides his horse alongside.

Int. Wagon - Day

Zumurrud and Alia ride in comfort. Alia looks out the window at Robert mounted on his horse. Zumurrud smiles and blocks her daughter's view with her hand.

Zumurrud

Eyes, eyes. What are you looking at?

Alia

He looks like a king, riding that horse. (she blushes)

Zumurrud

I agree. Keep your hopes high, he is a Muslim and a warrior.

Alia smiles and turns away as Robert's eyes notice hers. She blushes, suddenly awkward.

Ext. Damascus - Day

The caravan arrives at Saladin's palace.

Int. Hall outside Saladin's throne room - Day

Zumurrud enters Saladin's throne room while Robert and Alia wait just outside in the hall. Robert and alia meet eyes again, but this time their glance ends with a smile.

Saladin

(from inside the throne room)

Let them enter!

Int. Throne room - Day

Alia and Robert enter the throne room. Zumurrud stands next to her brother the sultan Saladin (49), also of Kurdish ancestry, a tall thin and severe man.

Robert and Alia

Assalam Alaikum.

Saladin

Walaikum Assalam. Welcome to Damascus, Robert of St. Albans. Your reputation travels before you: my soldiers spoke of your strengths in battle long ago. I am pleased that God has guided you to the right path.

Robert

I am delighted to meet a great leader like you. Do not look back to my past because it's now history. But you can count on my experience as a warrior to return Jerusalem to the people who worship God the one and only.

Saladin

And why are you so eager to join my army?

Robert

I regret my previous role, and I want to correct my past actions.

Saladin

An experienced warrior like you can lead an important portion of the army. We will see in the coming days what battle you can lead.

Robert

I am ready to be of service, your grace.

Ext. Caliphs palace - Night

Averroes and Yazeed arrive back in Seville.

Yazeed

See you tomorrow. Rest well my teacher.

Averroes

Same to you, young man.

Averroes turns toward his front door and his dog runs to greet him, blocking his entry and licking his hands.

Averroes bends down.

Averroes

Oh, you miss me my good friend. What a loyal creature!

Averroes pulls some dried meat he has brought from Marrakesh and gives it to his dog.

Int. Averroes chambers - Night

Averroes opens his front door, he enters his home, and the cats greet him as well. Rabab comes sleepily out of her bedroom.

Rabab

Father. I'm so glad you are safely home.

Averroes

Is everything alright? How are your courses? The translations?

Rabab shakes her head and smiles with affection and annoyance. She takes his bags and puts them down near the door, then circles around her father and pushes him towards his bedroom door.

Rabab

We will talk about all of that tomorrow father. Now you go directly to bed and have some rest.

Int. Damascus palace - Night

The wedding party of Alia and Robert. Singers and dancers perform the song Bali ma3ak.

Int. Palace bedroom - Night

As the wedding party continues the newlyweds shyly approach the bed which has been strewn with rose petals and surrounded by candles. Their shyness disappears as passion takes over.

Ext. Jerusalem battlefield - Day

Robert leads the Muslim army as they clash with crusaders. Robert swings his sword with vengeance and his former allies fall around him. Two generals of the crusaders look on as he kills their men.

Crusader general I

This English swine, son of a bitch.

Crusader general II

I have never trusted the templars, especially those coming from England. But this pathetic army he leads won't stand against ours.

Robert loses the battle.

Ext. Damascus - Day

Robert and his dozens of remaining men return to the palace in Damascus, defeated. Some bystanders, dressed in the clothing of the fundamentalists, mock his arrival.

Man in the crowd

The infidel will remain forever an infidel, an eternal loser.

Int. Damascus palace - Day

Alia rushes to her husband, tears of relief streaming from her eyes.

Int. Damascus palace throne room - Day

Saladin sits atop his throne. He greets one of the generals returning from battle.

Saladin

How was it?

General

We lost. I told you we did not send enough troops.

Saladin

(smiling sneakily)

I knew you would lose. Tell me, how was Robert?

General

He fought bravely. I have never seen such a commander, they had triple our number, but he had no fear.

Saladin

That's what I wanted to hear. He knows every corner of the holy city. He will be invaluable in planning the attack on Jerusalem.

Ext. Riverside - Day

Caption: 1187 AD

Abu Omar takes a siesta half naked near the river. A young man, Jaber (21) watches from behind a nearby rock. He is unable to control his desire. He approaches Abu Omar, coughing gently, but with no reaction. He reaches out and touches the older man on his chest. Abu Omar opens his eyes in surprise.

Abu Omar

Jaber! What are you doing here?

Jaber

(smiling)

It's such a sunny day. I thought you would like a massage.

Abu Omar looks at the young man, registering excitement in his face. The young man again touches Abu Omar's chest. No objection. Abu Omar, suddenly overcome by years of celibacy, puts his left hand behind Jaber's head. They move closer until they kiss.

Int. Abu Omar's house - Night

Abu Omar and Um Omar dine together with Omar, Rawya and Ruqaya, who is no longer wearing a head scarf.

Int. Bedroom - Night

Omar helps his father put his mother to bed and then leaves the room. Um Omar lays in bed, Abu Omar holds her hand, sitting beside her.

Um Omar

You look very happy today. (winking at her husband) what's going on, you found a woman!

Abu Omar

No. You read too much into my mood lately. I can promise that you will forever be the only woman in my life.

Int. House of Khalid - Night

A gathering of zealots in the house of the arrested ex-imam Khalid.

Zealot I

The problem is that Averroes is very popular among the people of Andalusia.

Zealot II

We must find a way to destroy the bond between him and the caliph.

Thats the key to getting rid of his influence. He doesn't allow our popularity to grow, and we cannot continue like this. Our friends are doing well in the Ayyubid state. It's time we followed suit and took control here.

Ext. Riverside - Day

An early morning ride along the riverside, three of the zealots from the night before see Abu Omar and Jaber across the river. The two lovers are entwined, hidden from the world in the reeds. The zealots watch long enough to perceive what is happening, then charge across the river.

They pull the old man savagely by his hair and tie him and the young man to horses using ropes. They drag them back to the city.

Ext. Seville city gates - Day

Averroes and two guards are returning from a trip and come across the men dragging Abu Omar and Jaber behind their horses. Shocked Averroes yells out.

Averroes

(to his guards)

What is this? Arrest those men!

The zealots see the guards come their way. They cut the ropes and ride away at top speed. Averroes rushes to the bleeding men. He picks up Abu Omar in his arms while a guard tends to Jaber.

Averroes

(to Abu Omar)

You are in a bad state. Don't speak. (to the other guard) bring a wagon and some help quickly! We cannot put him on a horse.

Abu Omar's face covered with blood, tears flow from his eyes.

Abu Omar

I am so sorry. Please forgive me. Let my family forgive me. I couldn't stop myself.

Averroes

Shush... You shouldn't speak. It's not good if there is internal bleeding. No matter what you have done, it does not justify such cruelty.

Abu Omar

Please promise me that you will still allow my son to marry your daughter. He loves her so much. Oh my god what have I done!

Averroes

Please stop talking now. You have my word that they will marry. She loves him too.

Abu Omar smiles in relief. He grasps Averroes' hand in gratitude then dies.

Tears flood Averroes' face. He lays the body gently down. Jaber knelt beside Abu Omar, sobbing at the loss of his love.

The guard returns with two doctors and a wagon.

Averroes

It's too late for the old man. Please take care of Jaber.

The doctors gently pick up the sobbing Jaber and lead him to the wagon. Averroes turns to the guard.

Averroes

Do you know the identity of the three who attacked
them?

Guard

yes.

Averroes

I want them to be arrested by tomorrow morning.
Please inform Abu Omar's family... Or rather I will go
to them myself. Just tell Jaber's mother that her son is
in critical condition.

The guard and the doctors depart towards the city,
bringing the body with them.

Averroes sits on the side of the road, staring at the
walls of Seville, this paradise he has created.

Int. Amphitheater - Day

Averroes stands in the center; the seats are filled with
citizens.

Averroes

Ladies and gentlemen, three barbaric individuals
have tortured and murdered Abu Omar Alansari
because he was seen in a moment of intimacy with
Jaber ben Muhammad. The families of the three
accused are calling for their release because they

claim the death of a homosexual man is justified according to law. I would like to hear the opinion of the magistrates.

Abu Utaiba

It's very clear in the Quran that God forbids sodomy. God punished the people of lot because of sexual encounters among the men. Therefor I see that our three brothers did the right thing. This is the only way to preserve our society from this disease and protect our youth from depraved people like that dirty old man.

The faces of Omar and Rawya become red with anger and humiliation.

Averroes

But the story of Lot took place in another era. The world has changed. The Quran states clearly that what was before Moses is different from what came after him. The verse says "that was a nation which has passed on. It will have [the consequence of] what it earned, and you will have what you have earned. And you will not be asked about what they used to do. " We cannot judge ourselves on the cultural context of another era. Society's rules have changed and that's why homosexuality is no longer considered a grave sin.

Another magistrate

I guess the old man has already been brought to justice. However, I think the young lad still has time to change his course. About the three men I think a short-term sentence could be possible, but I personally wouldn't bother even to jail them.

Averroes

Does anyone in this room want to add anything?

Silence.

Averroes

I will read the court decision shortly.

Averroes exits the amphitheater. The room erupts in chatter. Omar and Rawya sit miserably in the stands. Averroes finally returns, verdict in hand.

Averroes

We have here a deeply moving social story that ended in the horrible violent death of a member of our society. Abu Omar was one of the kindest souls that I have ever known. He was loyal to his wife, and I know that he refused to marry to a second woman after Um

Omar fell ill and became handicapped years ago. I am a little bit younger than Abu Omar and I am a widower, but yes, I can tell you from my own experience that man's sexual desire may diminish but does not die as he ages, so I am not at all surprised by what occurred between him and Jaber.

Jaber also has his own difficult life story. He is the only son of a widow, his father died before he was born. His mother is a very caring lady, but of course she can't fill the empty space of a father, or an older brother for her beloved son. And yet sometimes we simply cannot explain away the basic sexual desires of each individual. I ask you to return to this verse in Surat Albaqara "And the two men, who commit it among you, dishonor them both. But if they repent and correct themselves, leave them alone. " So, it's clear there is chance to repent and there is no call to kill them or torture them. But what's more, love knows no gender. True love never causes harm, and why should we condemn it? And have you forgotten that in the afterlife, God in his own words admits that in paradise there are young men who are more beautiful than diamonds. From Surat Alwaqiaa "there will circulate among them young men made eternal. "

And Surat Alinsan adds "when you see these men, you would feel like you are seeing scattered pearls".

So, it's perfectly clear that the Quran brought new light to homosexuality. It's not completely refused as it was before.

And since we do have in our hands a simple case of body attraction, admiration of old and young, and just an oral type of sexual activity, I announce that I found the three men guilty of torturing and murdering an innocent old man and they will be jailed until further notice from the caliph.

Jaber will remain free, and I personally will follow his improvement closely.

Protests come from the courtroom.

Omar and Rawya hurry out quickly. Rabab tries to catch Omar's eye, but he avoids her.

Int. Abu Omar's house - Day

Omar and Rawya arrive home to find the body of their mother on the floor. She is dead. On her bed they find an empty bottle of the liquid medication that Omar gave her every day.

Omar and Rawya hold each other sobbing.

128

Rabab arrives and takes in the scene. She embraces the brother and sister.

Rabab

There is no need to feel humiliated about your father. I understand the situation.

Rawya notices a note on the pillow. She picks it up and reads aloud.

Rawya

My dears Rawya and Omar, I am sorry because I had to leave you alone, but you are now grown, and you don't need me to add to your burden. Don't think that I decided to go because I am angry at your father or embarrassed by his last intimate encounter. No, not at all. Your father is a great man, he is the kindest soul I have ever known. I am going to him to tell him I love him. That we, his family, love him, and he need not be ashamed. I go in haste because I do not want him to suffer even one moment thinking that he has lost our respect and love. Enjoy your lives my children and remember to always trust in God. His love is truly boundless. God bless you. Goodbye.

The three embrace again, crying but with renewed peace.

Ext. Jerusalem battlefield - Day

Saladin and Robert lead the siege to the crusader-occupied Jerusalem. The city falls and the crusaders surrender.

Int. Damascus palace - Day

Alia is in labor.

Int. Random House - Day

A young man, and assassin, finishes his prayer. In the room are images of the 12 descendants of the prophet. He grabs a Christian monks' cloak and leaves out the front door.

Ext. Jerusalem battlefield - Day

The army of Saladin and Robert enters the city. Citizens of the city greet their liberators. Suddenly the assassin disguised as the monk attacks Robert and stabs him directly in the heart. Robert falls to the ground; Saladin gathers him in his arms as chaos erupts around them. The assassin swallows poison and dies, foaming at the mouth as the soldiers arrest him.

There is screaming, chaos, and the cries of a newborn baby.

Int. Damascus palace - Day

Alia as a beaming new mother holds her new boy, exhausted from labor. He cries a strong cry.

Ext. La Giralda square - Dawn

A large group of conservative imams arrives on Friday morning to Andalusia bringing them news of the conquest of Jerusalem.

Imams {shouting}

Saladin has conquered Jerusalem! God is great!

Int. Averroes chambers - Day

Averroes, Rabab and David sit with Camilla, comforting her as she cries over the news of Robert's death.

Camilla

All of my family is gone now.

David

You have me. I will never leave your side.

Averroes

We are your family. And there is one more piece of news I did not tell you. Robert married before he died. And his wife has given birth to a little boy. Your nephew.

Hope momentarily appears on Camilla's face before she starts crying again. Rabab takes her to her room.

Int. Mosque - Day

Abdul Darr (50) one of the extremist imams is standing at the front of the room, getting ready to make a speech before the Friday prayer. The room is filled with the Muslim citizens of Seville, a decidedly less conservative bunch, judging by their clothes and easy demeanor.

Averroes and Yazeed sit among the crowd.

Yazeed

I don't know why you would allow this foreigner to speak when he's just arrived. He doesn't look like the friendliest character to me.

Averroes

I don't want confrontations with them from the outset. They are not only here for a visit. They are here on a mission, and I have allowed him to speak so that I can read what between the lines of he says.

Abdul Darr

Bismillah Alrahman Alraheem. My name is Abdul Darr Azzam. I come to you from al-Azhar Mosque in Cairo, and I am here today to announce that God has blessed his true believers, our Muslim brothers, in our biggest victory. Jerusalem now belongs to us!

His colleagues attempt to rally the crowd by shouting victoriously.

Conservative imams

Allahu Akbar! Allahu Akbar!

To their surprise there is little reaction from the citizens of Seville.

Abdul Darr

From tomorrow there will be a religious course held every evening here at the mosque. I encourage you all to attend so you can learn the true message of Islam!

Ext. La Giralda square - Day - Continuous

Averroes and Yazeed exit the mosque, speaking quietly to each other.

Averroes

This is what I was afraid of.

Yazeed

They are indeed dangerous. What are we going to do about it?

Averroes

These are the people Robert fought and died for. I warned him but he had his own path to follow. Now that they have their Jerusalem and are drunk on their conquest, they have come to force their laws on us. How nice and luminous would our future be with these fools at the helm.

Yazeed

We must make sure that does not happen.

Averroes

I have no authority to forbid imams certified by al-Azhar from preaching here. Such a decision can only be made by the caliph. If he doesn't put limits on them, we will have to sit and watch them spread their disease. I have always seen al-Azhar central mosque as a threat to the future of Islam. It's barely 100 years old but it's gaining influence. These people will block the light and spread darkness. They will enslave people and take away their freedoms. They will suck life and spread their culture of hate and death. It's as if they were taking lessons from the papacy itself.

Yazeed

Shall we send a messenger to the caliph?

Averroes

He will not return from Africa before he is sure the Almoravids are under control. I don't think he'll take our concerns seriously.

Ext. Seville streets - Day

Time passes. The new arrivals quickly begin to bring down their interpretation of Islamic law. They force a group of women to cover their hair, beating them when they resist.

Int. Cafe - Night

The young imams break musical instruments in a lively cafe.

Int. Mosque - Day

Neat rows of young zealot converts fill the aisles of the mosque. No more idle chatter, they all read from books distributed by Al-Azhar.

Int. Lecture hall - Day

Averroes looks fatigued and has aged. He sits in front of his lecture hall, but the room is filled with only a fraction of the students who used to come to his courses.

Ext. Battlefield - Day

Abu Yusuf, returned from Africa, leads his soldiers to battle against the Christians.

Int. Dungeons - Day

Torture of prisoners of war: Christians by Muslims and Muslims by Christians.

Ext. La Giralda square - Day

A new solemnity hangs over the city square. Where there was chaos and brilliance there is now a somber mood, people moving robotically, women covered. Flowers are scattered, streets have become dirty as the population has lost interest in cleaning up the public space.

Int. Caliphs palace throne room - Day

Averroes is arguing fiercely with the caliph.

Averroes

Treating prisoners of war so horrendously is not acceptable by any divine law.

Caliph

They are doing worse to our soldiers they hold captive.

Averroes

We should treat them the way we would like to be treated. I am telling you clearly, I do not want any captive to be sold slaves here in Andalusia. And if I see one, I will leave, and you will not see my face again. We in Andalusia are above such barbarism.

Caliph

Leave wars to me, wise man. You continue to look after social matters.

Averroes

I want you to make peace with your northern enemies. God would bless such a move. Enough bloodshed.

Caliph

If you are not a wolf, the wolves will eat you. We cannot stop fighting if they continue attacking us. God justifies wars against the non-believers.

Averroes

Non-believers? Who are we to judge the faithful from the infidel? Look at me and listen carefully. Wars are never blessed by God. Go the verses of the Quran which I call "the basics of the connections between god and his creatures. " You will see. "And [mention], when your lord said to the angels, indeed, I will make upon the earth a successive authority. They said, will you place upon it one who causes corruption therein and sheds blood. While we declare your praise and sanctify you? God said; indeed, I know that which you do not know."

Caliph

What does this have to do with us now?

Averroes

Angels protested to God, asking him why he would give authority on earth to human beings who will spread violence and bloodshed. God answered that "no, these creatures would be full of knowledge and understanding. " So, what are you doing Muhammad and Jesus followers today, other than sectarian violence among yourselves, and chaos wherever you go! What path are you following? God clearly calls for peace, but you keep fighting each other and you disappoint him.

Caliph aka Abu Yusuf

Other verses call for war, wise man. How about when he says, fight them, Allah will punish them by your hand and will disgrace them and give you victory over them and satisfy the breasts of a believing people.

Averroes

This message was given at a time when ignorance reigned, and people were still making sacrifices to the gods. Now the entire world knows of God, each person is free to pick the faith he wants. And there are some global verses in this context: there shall be no compulsion in religion. Another verse says "invite (them) to the way of your lord by wisdom and good instruction and argue with them in a way that is best. " And that's what I and the other savants are trying to do. Peace is more powerful than war. Words conquer more effectively than swords. God taught the man with pen. The first verse in the Quran is read, not kill.

Ext. Hilltop - Day

The caliph and Alfonso VIII, each with their armies behind them, are atop a hill at the border between the Almohad and the Castilian kingdoms. They sign a truce.

Int. Toledo royal palace - Day

Toledo 1194: palace of the Spanish king Alfonso VIII.

Eleanor (37) is with her husband Alfonso VIII (40) on the balcony.

Eleanor

I don't think it's wise to attack the Muslim towns now. The truce is not yet over.

Alfonso VIII

Don't worry. The Calif is in Africa. It's time to test them. The pope has ordered a massive invasion to avenge our defeat in Jerusalem.

Eleanor

You will need the help the other kingdoms. Do you think they will obey the pope's orders and join the invasion?

Alfonso VIII

Our biggest advantage is the element of surprise. Yet I won't order such a massive attack while the truce with the Almohad is still valid. The small attack I am sending now is to test the water and send a message that the truce is over. The invasion will not take place before next year. I can't trust the kings around me, especially now with the son of my aunt holding a grudge against me.

Eleanor

You see, I told you to allow your own physician to look after Pedro, but you left him to struggle from one physician to another. I wouldn't be surprised if he turns against you.

Ext. Town - Day

Castilian soldiers ride through a town spreading horror and chaos inside the northern line of the Almohad kingdom.

Ext. Cordoba - Day

A wagon enters Cordoba, in it a very sick man.

Driver

We need to see the best physician here.

Man

Here in cordoba the best is Abu Tayeb.

The man sits on the edge of the wagon and guides at Abu Tayeb's clinic.

Int. Abu Tayeb's clinic - Day

Abu Tayeb's clinic is full of wounded people from the sudden attack. Abu Tayeb arranges a bed for the guest who is very ill.

Driver

He has had a pain in his stomach for over a year. And it's getting worse. No one in the north has managed to cure him.

Abu Tayeb

When the problem is hidden it is no easy task. Averroes will be here shortly because I can't deal alone with all these wounded people. The attack was unexpected since we had a truce with them.

Pedro

(while holding his stomach in pain)

That bastard Alfonso knows no oath.

Ext. Cordoba - Day

Abu Yahya and Averroes arrive at the head of hundreds of warriors to Cordoba.

Abu Yahya

I will strengthen the border lines. I think I should inform the caliph of what has happened.

Averroes

No dead people, they destroyed things and injured people. Wait for the time being, because I don't want to see a new outbreak of war. It could be just a stupid raid by their southern general.

Abu Yahya

I will follow your advice, but if something bad happens you will be responsible.

Averroes nods his head.

Int. Clinic - Day

Averroes is examining Pedro's body, Yazeed observes.

Averroes

Is there anything else?

Pedro

Yes. Lately I have had such pain when I defecate.

Averroes

I know what we are dealing with. Yet it will take months before you are fully cured.

Averroes

(to Yazeed) hand me my bag of medicines. I still have these precious bezoar stones, given to me by Avenzoar, may his soul rest in peace. One of these will ease your pain in a few days. Then we start another type of medication later.

Yazeed hands a cup of water to Averroes, who drops in a bezoar stone. He waits a little bit then hands it to Pedro.

Pedro

Thank you.

Averroes

You will be cured God willing.

Ext. Road - Night

Heavy rain in the winter. Averroes student Jose is riding a mule through the countryside from Calatrava to Seville with a satchel full of books. A group of Christian guards, from the order of Calatrava, stops and searches his belongings. They look through the books and quickly realize that they are unacceptable.

Guard

By the order of king Alfonso VIII, in the name of the catholic church, I declare these books to be heretical.

They set fire to them right there on the side of the road. The guard beats Jose, who falls from his mule into the mud. They ride off, taking the mule with them. Jose gathers himself and continues on his way, but not before checking his cloak to make sure that the most precious book is still tucked away safely inside the garment.

Int. Inn at Barchanona - Night

Rain pours outside. Sarah tears off her nun's costume and changes into her normal dress.

Ext. Street Barchanona - Night

Sarah runs out quickly and jumps into a wagon, throwing a little bag of coins to the driver.

Sarah

Please get me quickly to Seville.

The wagon leaves.

Int. Averroes chambers - Day

Early morning, Averroes is feeding his dog and cats in the garden. He hears the guard talking to someone.

Averroes

Who is it?

Sarah

It's me, Sarah.

Averroes

Please come in.

Guard

But the last orders from the caliph dictate that no Jews or Christians are allowed to enter the palace outside the time of studies or trials.

Averroes

Let her in. I'll take responsibility.

Sarah enters hurriedly. They embrace.

Sarah

What is it with these new restrictions?

Averroes

The situation is getting worse by the day since the victory in Jerusalem. Now these people think they are god's favorite. They have become proud and arrogant. I don't have the authority I once had. The extremist clerics are getting closer to the caliph. People like you are less and less welcome.

Sarah

I am also coming with dangerous news, your northern enemies are preparing a massive attack beyond imagination, they want to reconquer all of the Iberian lands. If you bring this information to the caliph, maybe you can win back your authority and his trust.

Averroes

Let us hope he will react wisely.

Sarah

Go to him now, because the threat is imminent.

Averroes

But Abu Yusuf is in Marrakesh. I must send a trustworthy messenger, and frankly my circle of trust has been so reduced. The only one I still have full confidence in is Yazeed.

Ext. Yazeed's house - Dawn

Averroes and Sarah knock on Yazeed's door.

Yazeed

(from inside) coming.

He opens the door yawning, surprised by his early morning visitors.

Averroes

Can we come in?

Yazeed

Yes of course.

Int. Yazeed's home - Day

They enter.

Yazeed

Forgive me, the room is not tidy. You know I have so much work these days.

He moves quickly inside as he tries to hide some item near his bed, he throws a cover at it. Sarah takes a seat, but Averroes curiously approaches Yazeed who is trying block his view. Averroes can only see a corner of a thick paper under the cover. He moves his blushing student gently aside and pulls out the paper to discover a drawing of himself. Averroes smiles kindly.

Averroes

You fool.

Yazeed looks shyly to the ground.

Sarah

(smiling)

A great drawing; it looks exactly like you Averroes!

Averroes returns the drawing to its place. He stands mutely waiting for the embarrassed Yazeed to meet his eyes. Yazeed slowly looks up to see Averroes reaction. His master is staring at him with a beautiful respectful smile. After a moment Averroes hugs him tightly.

Averroes

You are very dear indeed.

We have got an urgent mission for you. You must travel to Rabat to inform the caliph that the Christian armies are preparing a massive attack. We need his African army if he wants to defend Andalusia.

Yazeed

I am ready. How can I refuse to defend your world?

Ext. Seville battlefields - Day

The beginning of summer and armies gather on both sides. The Christian army gathers at the northern border of Andalusia. The Almohad army arrives from all over the kingdom to Seville.

Int. Averroes chambers - Night

Averroes sits writing. A knock at the door, and Jose enters muddied from the long journey. He collapses on his knees, but he is smiling.

Jose

The Amorite book you need for translation.

Averroes rushes to him, helping him up and placing the book on the table.

Int. Caliphs palace - Day

Averroes introduces Pedro to the caliph.

Averroes

This is Pedro the noble man from Leon, he came here ill, and we succeeded in curing him.

Pedro

I will gladly participate with you in this battle against Alfonso, the son of my uncle.

Caliph

(smiles)

You know very well the Castilian army; you will be of great help in planning our attack.

Pedro

I will gather my cavalry shortly and we will meet again in Cordoba.

Pedro leaves. Rabab passes in the hall. Abu Yusuf calls her.

Abu Yusuf

Rabab! This is a chance for me to talk to you while your father is here. (holding her arm, looking into her eyes) you are a very beautiful lady, and I would be proud if you agreed to be my second wife.

Confusion appears on Rabab's face. Averroes remains silent.

Rabab

You are the bravest man in the world and every woman would love of having you as a husband.

Caliph

(beaming)

Wonderful! We will make arrangements after I return from the war.

Rabab

Good luck your grace.

An awkward moment passes, and Averroes rescues his daughter by changing the subject.

Averroes

Have you finished reading Alhazen's book?

Rabab

No not yet. Please excuse me.

She leaves.

Caliph

As you see Alfonso didn't respect the truce. So, am I right to go to war this time?

Averroes

Yes, this time, they started it. And you are doing what you should do.

Ext. Cordoba battlefield - Day

Cordoba June 30, 1195. Local governors of Andalusian cities reinforce the main army. Pedro Fernandez de Castro joins his Christian cavalry with the Almohad army. Abu Yusuf and the armies move out of Cordoba.

Ext. Mountain pass - Day

They cross the pass of Muradal and advance through the plain of Salvatierra.

Ext. Hills - Day

A cavalry detachment of the order of Calatrava, scouts Almohad army, attempting to assess its strength and leadership.

A detachment of Muslim scouts surrounds them and attacks. A few escaped and supplied information to the Castilian king.

Int. Toledo castle throne room - Day

One of the cavalry knights brings reconnaissance to king Alfonso VIII.

Cavalry knight

I don't know how they found out about the attack, but they seem more than ready for war, your highness.

Alfonso

In that case, I will not wait for reinforcements. We will attack in a fortnight.

Ext. Hills of Alarcos - Day

The combined armies of Alfonso VIII march towards Alarcos.

Int. Averroes chambers/garden - Day

Averroes looks out his window into the garden, where Rabab and Omar are speaking intensely. Averroes turns from the window and wipes a tear from his eye. He picks up his cat and pets it.

Ext. Alarcos battlefield - Day

Caption: Wednesday, July 18, 1195

The Almohad army is in formation for battle around a small hill called la cabeza, close to Alarcos. The caliph passes by the factions of his giant army. He clashes swords in solidarity with Abu Yahya who is at the head of a very strong vanguard. In the first lines are Bani Marin volunteers. Second in line are archers and Zenata tribe. Third on the hill itself, Abu Yahya with flags of Almohads and his personal guard, from the Hintata tribe. To the left the Arab faction; and to the right, the Andalusian forces.

Abu Yusuf returns to command from the rear guard, which is comprised of the elite Almohad forces and a strong guard of black slaves.

Ext. Hills of Alarcos - Day

On the other side Alfonso forms his cavalry into a compact body thousand strong. The fierce Diego Lopez de Haro leads the cavalry. Alfonso commands Diego.

Alfonso

Attack now. We must shatter the enemy with our first charge. I will follow the infantry and the elite forces.

The Castilian cavalry charge into the heart of the Almohad joint army. The knights crash through their rivals in the middle and disperse the Zanattas and Bani Marin; then charge uphill to where the main Almohad army is standing.

Abu Yahya is killed, and the Hintatas are exterminated. Most of knights turn to their left and after a fierce struggle they route the Andalusian forces.

Under intense heat, fatigue and missiles take their toll on the armored Castilian knights.

The Arab right-wing circles around the Castilian flank and rear; at this point the Almohad elite forces attack, with the caliph himself clearly visible in the front ranks. Finally, the Castilian knights are almost completely surrounded.

Alfonso advances with all his remaining forces into the battle, only to find himself assaulted from all sides, a rain of arrows falling around him.

Alfonso's bodyguards protect him. Alfonso flees towards Toledo.

The special Almohad forces destroy the Castilian infantry, together with most of the elite knights who had supported them.

The lord of Vizcaya (Diego) tries to force his way through the ring of enemy forces, but finally he seeks refuge in the unfinished fortress of Alarcos with his few remaining cavalry.

The fortress is surrounded by the Almohad forces.

Civilians are trapped inside, half of them women and children.

Abu Yusuf

(to Pedro)

Go inside and demand surrender.

Int. Alarcos fortress - Day

Pedro enters the castle and talks to Diego

Pedro

Alfonso fled instead of standing by you. It's best if you surrender, Diego.

Diego

I do if you guarantee I leave unharmed

Pedro

Count it done.

Diego agrees and surrenders the city.

Ext. Hills of Alarcos - Day

The embattled Castilian army retreats across the hills.

Int. Averroes chambers - Day

Rabab and Averroes sit in her room.

Averroes

You love Omar. You marry him, end of story. Forget about the caliph.

Rabab

(in tears)

But you know his mind. He will get angry, and that could harm your position.

Averroes

I will be fine. Don't worry about me, now you two marry and leave Almohad lands for good before Abu Yusuf's return. This is your only chance.

Rabab

What do you mean "for good? " I can't live without you.

Averroes

You have to start your own life now. Omar loves you as much as I do. Don't worry about me, I will be fine. He hugs her tight with tears.

Rabab

Why don't you come with us?

Averroes

This is my place and here lies my duty.

Int. Toledo royal palace - Day

Eleanor

I told you to wait for the aid of the other kings.

Alfonso angrily gathers some clothes and leaves the palace without answering his wife.

Ext. Hilltop - Dusk

Alfonso sitting alone and crying from anger in front of a cross.

Int. Caliphs palace - Day

Averroes holds the hands of Rabab and Omar marrying them in a secret ceremony.

Ext. La Giralda square - Day

Omar sits in the driver's seat of a wagon, in it are Rabab and his sister Rawya. Rabab hugs Averroes again.

Rabab

I hope we will see each other again.

Averroes

God willing. Perhaps one day I will travel to Egypt. Peace be with you and God bless you. Good luck and goodbye.

Averroes cries alone as chariot leaves.

Ext. La Giralda square - Day

The people of Seville have gathered to celebrate the return of the caliph Abu Yusuf. They call him in a victorious celebration, "al Mansour"! The victorious by God! " Groups of zealots are among the crowd.

Averroes welcomes the caliph, who hugs him with joy. The zealots look on at this reunion with disapproval and envy. Abdul Darr, judge Abu Utaiba and the former imam Khalid, stand amongst the crowd, speaking quietly.

Khalid

We must drive a separation between them.

Abu Utaiba

The caliph is arrogant. If we expose Averroes' popularity to him, we will bruise his ego and he may begin to hate him.

Abdul Darr

Fortunately, some of his students have understood our message. I know of one who doesn't agree with him on many topics.

He looks across the crowd at the abundance of new young converts to their extremist ideologies. Hussein stands among them.

Int. Caliphs palace hammam - Day

Averroes massaging the caliph.

Caliph

Where is Rabab? I haven't seen her yet.

Averroes

She is away, Almansour. She left with a group of friends to conduct some scientific experiments.

Caliph

Damn. I need a wife here in Andalusia and your daughter is the best choice for me.

Averroes

Forgive me and forgive her. She was unable to predict when the war would end. She just left yesterday.

The caliph unhappily turns onto his stomach and holds his arm out for Averroes to massage it.

Caliph

I am relocating tomorrow to Cordoba, and I will stay there for a while.

Int. Lecture hall - Day

Students gather, though not as many as before. Among them is Hussein, who has regularly been attending lectures.

Yazeed

The point where religions, especially Islam and Judaism differ clearly from the ancient Greek religion is that we worship one god while they many gods, each with specific abilities and tasks.

Hussein

And for that reason, I don't really understand why you keep trying to reconcile the philosophy of Plato and Aristotle with our religion. They have nothing in common.

Averroes

To master this topic, Hussein, the religious thinker must make a preliminary study of logic, just as the lawyer must study legal reasoning. This is no more heretical in one case than in the other. And logic must be learned from the ancient masters, regardless of the fact that they were not Muslims.

Hussein

But they don't believe in the oneness of God and that's crucial for us because we were asked by the Quran not to take the infidels as our masters.

163

Averroes

That would be alright if we know for certain that these masters used to believe in many gods or only in one. In some books both Aristotle and Plato mention god in the singular and some other sources attribute to them quotes about gods in plural. There is nothing that can prove to us what they really believed. Here we must use logic to analyze what we received from them and to take what we agree with and refuse what appears illogical for us, and then explain why. This is the work I have been doing for the last two decades.

Dalia

But there is archeological evidence in their lands which shows they worshiped many gods.

Averroes

That is true. But one day in the future people will look back on our time and they will say Muslims believed in this or in that in general, but that does not mean that Yazeed or I held the same beliefs. There is always room for individuality when it comes to our faiths.

(opening a book)

However, in my new book I have analyzed pagan belief in ancient civilizations to find out how Jesus came to be worshiped as a god. When we look at Greek and roman mythology, we find that many leaders were made gods after their death. This is strikingly similar to Jesus divine story.

This was common practice in old times.

What's more I am convinced that there is a divine message in that claim: a human being's duty is to achieve great things in order to manifest godlike qualities. But people altered it for their own comfort so that any leader can go and win some battles or build some cities in order to become a god.

Yazeed

How do we explain the major gods then, in both Greek and Roman beliefs?

Averroes

Either they are a complete myth, or they are some angels that performed miracles and came to be worshiped by the people as gods. And in this fashion, it was shown that Venus was among the gods. Zeus and others too.

End of lesson. Students leave. Others linger, including Hussein. He pretends to be engrossed in a book while he listens to Averroes and Yazeed nearby.

Yazeed

Give me the new book and I'll start copying it.

Averroes

No rush. It's better if we focus on the translation of the Amorite book.

Yazeed

Yes, I've begun and already I'm finding many important passages.

Hussein

I'm sorry for disturbing your conversation but I would gladly attempt the copying, master.

Averroes

I'm so happy that you are eager to gain understanding of the connection between philosophy and religion! Show me your handwriting.

Hussein writes a line and hands the paper to Averroes.

Averroes

It looks good to me. It would be kind of you and a great service.

Averroes gives the book to Hussein, along with a few empty books to copy it into.

Int. La Giralda mosque - Night

Hussein rushes into the zealots meeting, book in hand. Among the attendees are Khalid, Abdul Darr and Abu Utaiba.

Hussein

We have got the bastard. He recently finished a book on Greek mythologies and our religion. There is a part in it that explains why the Greeks worshiped many gods instead of one.

Khalid

And how would that help us?

Hussein

The book is still new and has not yet been copied. We only have to remove some lines from it and keep lines such as "Jupiter was god or Venus" or anything of the sort. We show it to Almansour and tell him that Averroes is promoting the Greek gods instead of the one and only god.

Abdul Darr

Brilliant idea. But how can we remove the lines? That will look suspicious.

Hussein

We can get the book wet and words will become unreadable. Since the text is full of ancient deities; it will give the caliph the impression that it's really something suspicious. Also, Averroes handwriting is well known so he can't argue his way out of this.

Abu Utaiba

A smart boy.

Hussein

Since the book is new, we can also claim that it was a secret document which we found in his desk. Averroes will try to defend himself, but no copies have been made.

Abdul Darr

We must act quickly then, before it gets copied.

The men's eyes widen as Hussein pulls the only copy from his satchel.

Int. Cordoba palace - Day

Abdul Darr, Khalid and Hussein are talking to the
caliph and showing him papers from the book of
Averroes. They leave. The caliph turns to the guards

Caliph

Bring me Averroes here at once.

Ext. Cordoba - Day

Averroes, Camilla, and Sarah ride in two wagons
driven by Yazeed and David, surrounded by guards.

Int. Cordoba palace - Day

The throne room of the new palace, Averroes and the
caliph speak quietly.

Caliph

I have received some serious accusations against you.

Averroes

Against me?? Why? What have I done?

Caliph

You will soon know. See you at the trial tomorrow.

Averroes

Just tell me what the accusations are?

Caliph

You have gone too far in your writings. I can't allow anyone in my kingdom to promote paganism.

Averroes

Paganism? What the hell are you talking about? You know how devoted I am to my creator! How could you accuse me of such things?

The caliph does not reply, nor does he meet Averroes' eyes.

Averroes

Look me in the eye. Tell me what it is about? Is it because my daughter refuses to marry you? That is no reason to accuse me of such lies!

Caliph

So that's it, then! The truth is she doesn't want me?

Averroes

Yes. That is the truth. I did not want to upset you but now you must know. She has married Omar and they have left the kingdom together. Perhaps I should have left with them too.

Averroes turns his back on the caliph.

Averroes

I hoped to build the republic Plato dreamed of, here in Andalusia.

Caliph

The son of the old faggot is better than me? I am Almansour, victorious by God! You! Who are you Averroes? Nothing but a liar and an infidel. And no, Andalusia will not be a place for Plato and his pagan gods!

Int. Cordoba amphitheater - Day

People gather in the amphitheater for the trial of Averroes. Among them are Sarah, Yazeed, David, Camilla, and Dalia. Averroes stands accused and the caliph takes the place of the judge.

Hussein

Averroes has been recently lecturing on his theory about the harmony between religion and philosophy, but I find it blasphemy! It seemed he wants to pollute the minds of his students with pagan beliefs of the Greeks and promote the idea of the existence of many gods. I took it upon myself to search secretly in his desk, and I found these papers written in his hand.

The content is not clear, but it includes many phrases speaking about the ancient gods of Athens and Rome.

Here, (pointing) he says "And Venus was one of the gods. " And in another line "Jupiter was the god of the sky and thunder. " There are many phrases like this. We do not need more proof than this, Almansour, that Averroes is a blasphemer and a pagan. Therefore, I ask you to punish him before he does any further harm to our society.

Caliph

Averroes. This is your handwriting, isn't it?

Averroes

Indeed. However, these phrases are taken out of their context. I gave this man my new book for him to make copies, and he has erased parts and used my writings against me. I thought he was a decent man. Luckily all of the other students were present as I was reading from this new book about how ancient civilizations appreciated the divine. I did this study not to promote their beliefs but to do more research and compare the past and the present in order to better deal with the future.

Averroes students erupt in protest.

Yazeed

I witnessed that Averroes handed his book to this man.

Other students

What Averroes is saying is true.

Khalid

These are his students. They should also be punished.

Caliph

Silence! Does anyone have anything to add? Averroes.

Averroes

I have never lied to you. Regarding what has passed between us recently, I can only say I respect freedom of choice. No matter what you decide, I accept it as I trust your judgment.

The crowd shouts in support of Averroes.

Caliph

(stands and reads)

After seeing the evidence written in the hand of the accused himself, and because I know that he entrusts the copying of his books to only his closest students, I cannot believe the claims they are making today. I see no reason to revive the old deities and to speak of them as gods. We should make it clear that there is no room in our Muslim lands for any ideology other than the Quran, the hadith, and Islamic law. I personally doubt too much the intention of Averroes, especially since he has many Jewish and Christian friends. I am worried that he might be planning something that would ruin our religion and corrupt it. Therefore, I give Averroes until tomorrow to leave our land and never return.

The crowd gasps.

Caliph

Silence! I strip him from the duty of supreme judge of Andalusia. And to prevent further pollution of our society, I order that all of the books in his library and the copies of his books be burned in all the cities and towns in our state.

Take him out of my sight!

Averroes

(yelling)

You cannot limit the omnipotence of God to one book and one prophet!

The guards grab Averroes and drag him from the amphitheater. He continues to yell.

Averroes

If the sea were ink for (writing) the words of my lord, the sea would be exhausted before the words of my lord were exhausted, even if we brought the like of it as a supplement! Scientists and thinkers are higher ranked than prophets in god's eye! The angel Gabriel told Muhammad to say, "My lord, increase me in knowledge! "

Caliph

(mocking)

So, you are taking on the prophet too? How dare you?

Abdul Darr

Muhammad is our only role model. He is our savior!

Trial ends, zealots celebrate. Citizens boo the decision.

Ext. Cordoba square - Sunset

A bonfire of books is already raging. Books are brought from libraries on foot, on horseback and on wagons. Zealots throw the books into the fire as it grows and grows.

Averroes and his friends leave the palace, guards walk close to them. He loses composure and explodes in tears. Yazeed, also in tears, tries to comfort his teacher.

Moderate people watching the scene with sadness mixed with anger while the extremist community shouts

Zealots

Allah Akbar. Muhammad is our only role model!

Ext. Spanish countryside - Night

Averroes and his students leave on wagons and horses. Guards stop following them after they pass Cordoba borders.

Ext. Lucena streets - Dawn

They arrive in the Jewish town of Lucena and go straight to the house of the mayor.

Int. Mayors home - Day

Sarah explains the situation to the mayor.

Mayor

They are welcome of course; they have been good to us. My sister Hadassa lives alone, and her house is empty since she lost her husband. I wonder if she could rent it to you.

Sarah

She doesn't have to move out if the house is big. Please ask her and let us know. We will be waiting.

Ext. Lucena streets - Day

Hadassa (40) arrives breathlessly to Averroes wagon.

Hadassah

I just can't believe my eyes. Averroes here in flesh and blood.

Averroes blushes. She takes him by the hand and leads him towards her home.

Hadassah

I don't want money. I'm the one who should pay you to live in my house, you and all of your dear friends. What an honor to have such a genius stay with me.

Averroes

We don't want to be a burden. I feel humbled by your generosity, but we can afford to pay your rent.

They enter her home.

Int. Hadassah's house - Night

People gather each night at Hadassah's home amongst Averroes and his students. The atmosphere is one of a festive salon, with lectures and music. The number of attendees grows with passing time.

Int. Synagogue - Day

The rabbi (50s) is worried as the number of people attending services is dwindling since Averroes arrival. He speaks with a group of conservative young religious scholars. Amos (29), a young and zealous scholar, listens with anger.

Amos

You should ask the mayor to expel this dangerous man from here.

Rabbi

Maybe you are right after all. We are losing more and more people as time passes. They are even refusing to speak with me on the torah and the Moshiach anymore. They say Averroes has made them understand the divine better than we have.

Amos

So, what are we going to do? Leave him in peace while our town loses its religion?

Rabbi

We can't force him out. The wealthiest people are his friends. But we must find a way to limit his influence.

Int. Hadassah's house - Day

Averroes is holding the book from Solomon's temple in his right hand, and the translation from Amorite in his left hand.

Averroes

(to Yazeed)

Now the translation to English has been finished. Though we're not sure of every word, this is the best we can do. The general meaning is clear, I think it was written by the prophet Abraham.

179

Yazeed

(taking the book)

I love this part about the messiah and the coming golden age of humanity when human beings will reach eternal life. Unfortunately, we can't make it happen now.

Averroes

Yes, it's fascinating. At least it proves a big deal of what we both believe in. The power of humanity.

Int. House of rabbi - Day

Rabbis are sitting at a lunch table.

Rabbi II

Jews from other regions are coming here to learn from him. His danger is becoming critical.

Rabbi

We must fight him with the same weapon he is using philosophy and reason. I have sent a messenger to Cairo.

Man

Cairo? What for?

Rabbi

We need Maimonides' help. He is the most brilliant savant among the Jews, and he serves the Ayyubid royal family. He is the only one who could crush Averroes' influence here. He hates Muhammad and doubts him as a true prophet. I am sure he wouldn't tolerate a Muslim scholar influencing the Jewish community.

Rabbi II

A great idea. Do you think he'll agree to come?

Rabbi

We can only hope. It's now been two months since the messenger left.

Int. Cairo palace - Day

Maimonides, palace physician, is massaging al-Aziz (28) the young son of Saladin, inheritor of the throne of Egypt, ruler of the Ayyubid kingdom of Cairo. Maimonides finishes and bids goodbye, exiting to the hall.

Int. Cairo palace hall - Day - Continuous

A servant approaches him. Zumurrud is coming down the hallway.

Servant

A messenger has come from Andalusia.

Maimonides

For me?!

The servant nods.

Maimonides

Let him in please.

Zumurrud, having heard them speaking of Andalusia, stops to listen. The messenger arrives.

Messenger

We need your help.

Maimonides

Yes?

Messenger

(looking at Zumurrud)

We must talk in private.

Zumurrud moves on.

Messenger

I come from Lucena near Cordoba. Averroes, the former supreme judge of Andalusia has taken over our town. He is preaching his false message to our citizens... And they are leaving the synagogue!

Maimonides

He is a great savant, but that does not mean that what he says is the truth. No jew should abandon the torah.

Int. Cairo palace throne room- Day

Maimonides enters to see the prince al-Aziz who is sitting with his aunt Zumurrud and her daughter Alia. Robert's child Imad (9) is play-sword fighting with another young boy.

Maimonides

Assalam Alaikom mawlay alAmir. I have received an urgent message from my family in Andalusia. I feel I should respond to their request.

AL Aziz

(looking to his Zumurrud) what do you think?

Zumurrud

This messenger is here from Andalusia?

Maimonides

Yes.

Zumurrud

Can I speak with him?

The messenger is brought in.

Zumurrud

How is Andalusia after the big victory against Castile?

Messenger

People from other beliefs are not as welcome as they used to be.

Zumurrud

How is that? Where is Averroes?

Messenger

Almansour burned all of his books and sent him into exile.

Zumurrud

My god! Why on earth? Thank you. You may leave.

The messenger is led away.

Zumurrud

184

I will go there with Maimonides.

Maimonides

(surprised) With pleasure!

Alia

I want to meet Averroes too. He was my husband's greatest influence.

Ext. Lucena streets - Day

Wagons of Maimonides and companions arrive in Lucena.

Int. Synagogue - Day

The rabbi welcomes Maimonides warmly but is surprised by the two members of the Ayyubid royal family, and their child.

Zumurrud

Thank you for welcoming us. We will not disturb you. We have come to see Averroes.

The rabbi, unable to hide his anger and frustration turns to a servant.

Rabbi

Guide them to the house.

They leave.

The rabbi and Maimonides walk through the synagogue as the rabbi explains the situation.

Int. Hadassah's house - Day

Zumurrud is escorted into Averroes study by Camilla.

Zumurrud

Assalam Alaikum. My name is Zumurrud AL Ayubi. I am the sister of Saladin. This is my daughter Alia and her son Imad. We have come from Cairo to see Averroes.

Averroes

My god. It is an honor to have such supporters as you.

Camilla suddenly realizes who these people are. She jumps forward.

Camilla

Are you Robert's wife? And you, his son?

Alia

Yes... And you must be...

Camilla embraces her and Imad.

Camilla

Yes! I am Camilla, the sister of Robert! Thank God for such a gift! What luck to meet you because we will soon return to England. This is my husband, David.

Ext. Evening dinner - Garden

Maimonides and Averroes dine together in a garden. They praise each other's ideas and writings.

Maimonides

I'm so glad to meet you in person because I was impressed by your works. But I must tell you that people here are annoyed by the fact that you're driving the citizens away from the torah. This must end.

Averroes

I do not call them to reject their religion, but they ask me questions and I answer them with the truth as I see it. If they are convinced by my answers, this is their choice. I am not forcing anyone. And I do not claim that my theories are proven facts.

Maimonides

Thank you for your lessons and for your attempt to guide our society. But from now on I can take your place.

Int. Maimonides house - Day

Crowds gather in Maimonides' house, spilling out onto the street.

Int. Hadassah's house - Day

Averroes, Yazeed and the Ayyubid visitors discuss his philosophies pleasantly. The townspeople are no longer present.

Int. Maimonides house - Day

Maimonides classes have gotten smaller, the rabbis watch over as the remaining townspeople look bored.

Int. Hadassah's house - Day

The townspeople have returned to hear Averroes' lessons.

Int. Maimonides house - Day

Maimonides explodes in anger as he's talking to the rabbi and other religious scholars.

Maimonides

This is impossible! I have never been humiliated in such a way. We must hold a public debate! The people will see who gives the more convincing answers!

Ext. Lucena public square - Day

Thousands gather from all regions to watch the debate between the two minds in the big square of Lucena. The mayor of the town is the mediator. Averroes and Maimonides stand opposite each other.

Mayor

We begin this debate as requested. The two savants face each other. I will state a topic, and each will state their opinion. (turning to the two opponents) are you ready?

Maimonides and Averroes nod.

Mayor

Muhammad.

Maimonides

He was either a false prophet, or a true prophet who was sent to test our faith. But I believe he was an insane man, a self-centered person like Jesus before him.

Averroes

Muhammad was a prophet of God. He was an honest man. Yet he was not educated, and so he sometimes fell into the trap of his own desires, and he committed mistakes like every other human being.

Mayor

Jesus.

Averroes

A prophet of God. He had high spirit and performed some miracles. He was an opportunity sent by God to humanity to stand united behind him and win their independence, but unfortunately, they weren't ready. Instead of coming together, they became more divided.

Maimonides

He was a sick man and a liar. He drove believers away from the torah and deceived them that he was the savior and the son of the almighty. The romans crucified him and proved he was just an ordinary man.

Mayor

Moses.

Maimonides

Most preeminent among the prophets. He was the savior of the children of Israel from the cruelty of the pharaoh. He received the torah directly from God and that's why we should follow him without question because his path is the only right path.

Averroes

(laughing)

Is that because your first name is also Moses?

The crowd laughs.

Averroes

Moses was an ordinary man who happened to commit a crime and killed an Egyptian. He repented to his creator who then made him a prophet and sent him with magical tools to rescue the children of Israel from Egypt.

Mayor

God

Averroes

The light of heavens and earth. The creator of our universe. The eternal. The source of all intelligence, wisdom and knowledge. The merciful and the almighty. He exists in each one of us through our spirits, souls and consciences.

Maimonides

God is not not-eternal. We don't know his exact form. He is aware of all of our deeds. We can know his characteristics by defining what can be attributed to him. Therefor since I ignore totally the essence of God, I prefer to say He is not ignorant instead of saying He is wise.

Mayor

Holy book.

Maimonides

There is only one holy book, and it is the torah of Moses. We must live by its rules and glorify our god.

Averroes

Every written book is holy in one way or another. I have read millions of words and in each volume, there is something, even if it is small, there is always something to learn. I do not attach myself to one specific book. The holy word in the eye of the public is the word of God. A part of the soul of God exists in each human being and that's why every human being can write the word of God if he is well connected with himself and his creator.

Mayor

The messiah.

Maimonides

The messiah or the savior, he is an awaited Jewish man who will unite humanity according to the torah, and he is a descendant of kind David and will inherit the throne of earth forever. I believe his name would be Moses.

Yazeed, the Amorite book in his hand. Averroes meets his eye, and a smile plays on his face. He turns back to Maimonides.

Averroes

Well, who knows, it might be you?

The last king is expected to be a man of wisdom and knowledge who will establish a connection with the creator even deeper than Abraham's. He will refuse to be categorized into any one religion. He could be born to any family regardless of the faith of his parents. He will rebel against all established religions carrying the flag of humanity. He will bring justice to everybody, and humanity will know its golden age. Therefore, God will give him the throne of earth forever. And there will be no more death, wars or diseases.

Crowd

Averroes. Averroes.

Ext. Road - Day

Camilla and David are sitting in their wagon, about to leave on the road going north to England. Imad, Zumurrud and Alia ride with them in a separate wagon. Averroes hands Camilla the Amorite book and its translation.

Averroes

Robert told me to make sure this was returned to the king of England. He said if king Henry is dead which the case is now, then you should give it to his consultant Ronald. He is a man of trust, and he knows best how to deal with the documents.

Camilla

Thank you very much. I will make sure they get into the right hands.

Averroes

Have a safe journey. It was a great pleasure to meet you all. Take care.

Wagons leave and disappear. Averroes and Yazeed are now alone talking among the trees near the road. They hear a noise from a field near them. Yazeed is the quickest to see a man targeting them with a bow and arrow. The assassin fires his arrow targeting Averroes, Yazeed quickly stands up protecting his teacher. The arrow penetrates his chest. The assassin runs away. Averroes kneels trying to rescue his friend as blood floods out of Yazeed's body. Yazeed smiles through his pain.

Yazeed

Thank God.

Averroes

(horrified) Don't talk.

Yazeed

Thank God, I always wished to die in your arms.

Averroes

Don't say that. You can't die.

Yazeed

I want to let you know. I love you.

Yazeed struggles to get closer. Averroes understands and kisses him on the lips. Yazeed dies. Averroes hugs him tightly crying out loud.

Averroes

No. God no. You were the future. You were everything. No.

Ext. Lucena square - Day

Averroes says his last goodbye and prays near Yazeed's body. One last kiss on the forehead.

Sarah

I managed to convince the guards of the city. They will allow us to bury the body as you wished near your wife at your family's cemetery in Cordoba".

Averroes

(lowers his head)

You have no idea how much I wish it was me.

Sarah comforts him then leaves with the chariot and the body to Cordoba.

Averroes cries until the chariot disappears.

He walks like a blind man to his house and Hadassah tries to comfort him as well.

Int. Averroes room - Day

Alone in a dark room, Averroes is completely devastated. He has let his beard grow long; he no longer sees his students. He spends his days remembering all he has lost, Andalusia, Yazeed, his dream.

A knock at the door. Maimonides enters and puts his hand on the shrunken Averroes.

Maimonides

I am here to apologies about that terrible incident. We are still chasing the assassin and he will be punished according to the torah which means death penalty.

Averroes

Don't kill him, give him a chance to repent and change course. I am sure Yazeed forgives him.

(sad laughter)

After all Yazeed's dream came true: he died in my arms.

Maimonides

I have to admit that you impressed me more in the debate than in your writings.

Averroes

My brotherly advice to you is to not imprison yourself in a specific category of race or religion. We are all brothers in one human family. No offense but there is no hidden meaning in the torah. You have to understand that the evolution of the human mind continues. Humanity is like any one of us, it was born as a little baby and then it gained experience, that's why it needs time to mature and become perfect. Do not attach too much value to the past because the best will always be in the future. We have just spoken about the death penalty; don't you find it strange that Moses himself who killed someone was forgiven and became prophet. So why did he later receive a message saying an eye for an eye. This is illogical.

Maimonides

I had not thought of that before.

Averroes

To understand things better you should never prejudge them, you must approach them in a neutral way. Read the torah not as a Jew, read the bible not as a Christian, read the Quran not as a Muslim. If we are just to obey a prophet and follow a book why we have been given minds?

Maimonides silently considers.

Int. Hadassah's house - Day

A messenger from Marrakesh arrives. Averroes' beard has grown long. He sits tired, hunched over a book. Hadassah also reads, content to be by the side of the weary master.

Messenger

Assalam Alaikom.

Averroes

(in a weak tired voice) Walaikum Assalam.

Messenger

Mulana Almansour sends his apologies. He wants you to return. He is in Marrakesh and facing troubles with the zealots.

Averroes

199

(smirks)

I am fine here. I have no desire to travel such a long distance just to see his arrogant ignorant persona. Tell him I accept his apologies and I forgive him, and I wish him all the best for the future in dealing with his internal problems.

Averroes suddenly, as if he received an injection that rejuvenated him, turns his head to continue the book he was reading. Without looking up he asks Hadassah:

Averroes

I feel a bit better today. What are you preparing for lunch?

Hadassah

I have all the herbs you like for a soup. And some falafel.

Averroes

That would be nice. I would like it well cooked.

Hadassah

Yes. I think your guest can have his lunch with us as well.

Averroes then turns towards the door